//////// NASCAR®

SECRET~

From the opening gree~ ~~ ~~ ~~yuna to the final checkered flag at Homestead, the competition will be fierce for the NASCAR Sprint Cup Series championship.

The **Grosso** family practically has engine oil in their veins. For them racing represents not just a way of life but a tradition that goes back to NASCAR's inception. Like all families, they also have a few skeletons to hide. What happens when someone peeks inside the closet becomes a matter that threatens to destroy them.

The **Murphys** have been supporting drivers in the pits for generations, despite a vendetta with the Grossos that's almost as old as NASCAR itself! But the Murphys have their own secrets... and a few indiscretions that could cost them everything.

The **Branches** are newcomers, and some would say upstarts. But as this affluent Texas family is further enmeshed in the world of NASCAR, they become just as embroiled in the intrigues on and off the track.

The **Motor Media Group** are the PR people responsible for the positive public perception of NASCAR's stars. They are the glue that repairs the damage. And more than anything, they feel the brunt of the backlash....

These NASCAR families have secrets to hide, and reputations to protect. This season will test them all.

Dear Reader,

The problem with secrets is that we eventually become their prisoners. The people in this story have secrets, long-hidden, shameful secrets—secrets that have the potential to destroy them and the people they love. Exposing secrets can be dangerous and painful.

I don't think it's a secret that NASCAR is a team sport. Writing a story as part of a continuity is like driving in NASCAR. You can't do it alone. I've been privileged, however, to have a fantastic team supporting me. Not just the other writers, who have been enormously generous with their time and ideas, but also the editors, who have kept us all on track!

To all of them I owe a special debt of gratitude and thanks for setting us on the winning course.

I hope you'll check out my Web site at www.kencasper.com.

Thank you,

Ken Casper

NASCAR

RUNNING ON EMPTY

Ken Casper

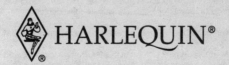

HARLEQUIN®

TORONTO • NEW YORK • LONDON
AMSTERDAM • PARIS • SYDNEY • HAMBURG
STOCKHOLM • ATHENS • TOKYO • MILAN • MADRID
PRAGUE • WARSAW • BUDAPEST • AUCKLAND

ISBN-13: 978-0-373-21797-7
ISBN-10:   0-373-21797-8

RUNNING ON EMPTY

Copyright © 2008 by Harlequin Books S.A.

Kenneth Casper is acknowledged as the author of this work.

NASCAR® and the NASCAR Library Collection® are registered trademarks of the National Association for Stock Car Auto Racing, Inc.

www.eHarlequin.com

Printed in U.S.A.

KEN CASPER

aka K.N. Casper, figures his writing career started back in the sixth grade when a teacher ordered him to write a "theme" explaining his misbehavior over the previous semester. To his teacher's chagrin, he enjoyed stringing just the right words together to justify his less than stellar performance. That's not to say he's been telling tall tales to get out of scrapes ever since, but…

Born and raised in New York City, Ken is now a transplanted Texan. He and Mary, his wife of thirty-plus years, own a horse farm in San Angelo. Along with their two dogs, six cats and eight horses—at last count!—they also board and breed horses and Mary teaches English riding. She's a therapeutic riding instructor for the handicapped, as well.

Life is never dull. Their two granddaughters visit several times a year and feel right at home with the Casper menagerie. Grandpa and Mimi do everything they can to make sure their visits will be lifelong fond memories. After all, isn't that what grandparents are for?

You can keep up with Ken and his books on his Web site at www.kencasper.com.

To Florence Domin
Who has always been there
Thanks for the memories

To Marsha Zinberg
and Tina Colombo
Thanks!

Speculation is running rampant about what, exactly, is going on with Hugo Murphy. The usually dependable crew chief has been rather distracted lately—*supposedly* with worry over his daughter's health problems, but word has it that he might have finally located his long-lost ex-wife.

PROLOGUE

"FROM PRELIMINARY TESTS, the donor match appears to be nearly perfect," Dr. Peterson assured Hugo Murphy. "Couldn't ask for better. I know this is wasted advice, but I'll say it anyway. Don't worry. Your daughter will be just fine."

The phone on the desk dinged discreetly. Peterson rolled his eyes and picked up the receiver. "Yes? No, no, I'll come out and look at it there." He replaced the instrument and climbed to his feet. "A minor crisis. I need to check something out front. I'll be back in just a minute." He left the examining room.

Hugo suddenly found himself alone. Kim was using the ladies' room across the hall. Wade Abraham, her fiancé, was outside on his cell phone. Hugo jumped up, made sure the office door was closed and stood over the desk. Kim's patient file lay there. He'd asked about the donor and been told the person wanted to remain anonymous. But he had to know. Nervously he opened the file.

All the old forms were held in place by a metal fastener. Only the newest additions were still loose. He flipped through them—the latest lab results with the local medical center's distinctive header—until he came to one that was clearly from another lab. He scanned it quickly, ignoring the medical data, which he didn't understand, and at last found a name at the bottom of the page: *Nancy Jean Smith.*

Hearing talk just outside the door, he frantically searched for and finally found an address, memorized it and tucked the papers back in place. He had his hands behind his back and was examining a color-coded diagram of the renal system tacked on the wall behind the desk when Kim entered the room.

"Where's Wade?" she asked.

"He received a call from his sister. He's outside talking to her now, and Dr. Peterson is—"

"Right here," Peterson said, coming up behind her.

Wade was right behind him. "Sorry," he mumbled, and returned to Kim's side as she sat down.

"Everything all right?" she asked him.

"Fine. I brought Sarah up to date and told her we'd meet her and Mom later," Wade replied. "They send their best."

Hugo watched his daughter's eyes soften as she squeezed her fiancé's hand. So much hope and so much uncertainty.

The next thirty minutes were filled with information. The surgeon explained in detail the compatibility issues and tests he'd be exploring in the week ahead in preparation for the transplant surgery: electrocardiograms, kidney-function tests and X-rays, cholesterol and blood-sugar levels, as well as a battery of surgical risk assessments. Kim had hoped to have the surgery quickly, but the doctor had ordered more tests and wanted her body more stabilized—she *was* a bit anemic—and had delayed the procedure. Through it all Hugo's mind kept wandering to the name of the "anonymous" donor. *Nancy Jean Smith.*

Not Sylvie Murphy or Sylvie Ketchum or any combination of those names.

Did that mean Nancy Jean Smith wasn't Sylvie? Not necessarily, though he had to admit it didn't seem very likely she was. Most people, including Kim, figured her mother was dead, but Hugo had never been able to convince himself of that. He didn't know what had happened to the woman he'd married, the woman who had disappeared from his life without a trace one afternoon thirty years ago, leaving behind her four-year-old daughter from a previous relationship for him to raise, but he didn't believe she was dead.

Was it possible Kim's anonymous donor was her own mother?

CHAPTER ONE

IT WAS WELL PAST twelve o'clock when they left Dr. Peterson's office. Kim had spent two days in the hospital last week after her collapse at the race track and had then been released as an outpatient. She was always positive in attitude, and her engagement to Wade and the news that a donor had come forward lifted her spirits even more. She wanted to have the surgery immediately, but as a scientist, understood the need for more tests.

Hugo was ecstatic. His daughter was finally going to get the transplant she required; unfortunately the surgery was still a week away. In the meantime he had to check out this Nancy Jean Smith woman. If it was Sylvie—

"Join us for lunch," Wade urged. "We have to make sure Kim eats."

She stuck out her tongue at him.

"You two go ahead," Hugo demurred. He had only one thing on his mind at the moment, and lunch wasn't it. He figured these two lovebirds would rather be alone, anyway.

"Come with us, Dad," Kim urged, and coiled her arm around his. He knew his protest was futile.

She suggested a well-known eatery, famous for its huge sandwiches and rich soups. Hugo followed her sports car in his SUV. Wade was driving. Kim was on her cell phone, probably giving her cousin Rachel the latest news. Justin, Rachel's brother, the driver of No. 448 in the NASCAR Sprint Cup Series, was in Winston-Salem today, doing a promo for his sponsor, Turn-Rite Tools. Kim would no doubt fill him in later, if Rachel hadn't already.

They were in luck when they arrived at the restaurant a few minutes later. The first wave of customers was clearing out, so they were seated immediately.

While they examined their menus, Kim steered the conversation to Wade's family back in Tennessee. She'd gotten to spend some time with them when they came up to the Bristol race, and she had fallen in love with the big clan. Sunday dinner at his mother's house, Wade said, rarely involved fewer than a dozen people.

Hugo, too, had once entertained notions of having a big family. Instead, he'd become a single father to three children, none of whom was he the biological father of, but whom he couldn't have loved more if he had been. They'd turned out okay, too, more than okay. He was proud of all of them.

Yet he'd never stopped waiting for Sylvie to come home.

He'd felt so helpless these past months, ever since Kim had been diagnosed with acute kidney failure— even more helpless than he had when her mother had walked out on him years ago, abandoning him and her child. He'd done everything he could to find Sylvie, but she had disappeared completely, vanished without a trace.

"I wish my surgery didn't have to be put off until next week," Kim said after they'd placed their orders. "I'm ready now. I want this to be over."

"We've waited this long," Wade reminded her. "A week is nothing, now that we know there's a donor available. Besides, the doc is right, the more time he has to run tests and prepare, the better."

"Well, the good news is that I'll be able to go to Martinsville this weekend," Kim commented.

"I don't think that's a good idea, honey," Hugo said. "You've collapsed twice at race tracks, last month at Kansas and last weekend at Charlotte."

"They were just accidents," she argued. "I let myself get carried away. It won't happen again. I'll be more careful."

"You scared the daylights out of us," Hugo countered. "For a few hours, we actually thought we might lose you. I don't want you taking another chance like that, especially right before surgery."

"He's right," Wade said. "It's too dangerous for you to go this weekend."

She frowned at her fiancé, then glared at her father.

"You can watch it on TV," Hugo said, "in air-conditioned comfort."

"Spoilsport," she said with a disappointed pout.

She toyed with the flatware at her place setting. "I asked Dr. Peterson's assistant this morning about the donor," she said. "He wouldn't tell me anything, said the person insisted on remaining anonymous."

As soon as Hugo had learned Kim needed a new kidney and he realized that neither he nor his niece and nephew were compatible donors—they were not biological relations and so their chances had been small to begin with—he'd hired another detective agency to find Sylvie. After thirty years of silence, the prospect seemed remote, and in fact, they'd come up dry, as had the previous investigators. He'd had no choice, though. He had to keep trying. He'd have done anything to save his precious daughter. At no point in Kim's life had she needed her mother more than she did now. She had a rare blood type, and Hugo remembered that Sylvie was AB negative, as well. If they were ever going to find a compatible kidney donor for Kim, Sylvie was the most likely candidate, he'd thought, the best hope, and maybe her last hope.

"He told me the same thing," Hugo said, aware of his daughter slanting a questioning glance at him. "You really can't blame the donor," he added. "If the press caught wind of this, they'd turn it into a circus, get in her face, hound her for interviews—"

"Her?" Kim's eyes lit and dimmed, almost as quickly. "You know it's a woman?"

Hugo didn't have to be a mind reader to know what his daughter was thinking or to recognize the forlorn hope he saw in her eyes. Should he tell her he'd sneaked a peek at the medical record and found the name Nancy Jean Smith and that he intended to check her out?

He decided not to. It could be another dead end— there had been so many of them over the years. He didn't want to hold out hope that maybe her mother had been found. He knew how devastated she always was when it turned out not to be true.

He shook his head. "Peterson's assistant referred to the donor as *she,* but when I questioned him about it, he claimed if the recipient were a man he would refer to the anonymous donor as *he.* The guy likes to play word games."

Wade reached over and took Kim's hand. "The

important thing, darling, is that someone has come forward."

She smiled at him, then frowned at her father. "I don't want it to be *her,* Dad. I don't know why. I can't explain it. But I don't." Her hand shook as she reached for her iced tea.

"Hey, calm down, Kim. No getting all worked up." Wade stroked her hand. "Doctor's orders."

"Don't you give it another thought, sweetheart," Hugo said in his most casual manner, grateful that their food had arrived. "Whoever the donor is wants to remain anonymous, so we'll just leave it that way."

But who exactly was Nancy Jean Smith?

IT WAS AFTER one o'clock when Hugo was finally able to break away. He loved his daughter and enjoyed her fiancé's company, but his attention had been elsewhere. He'd managed to eat half a club sandwich before he finally understood what it must be like for Kim to have to eat when she wasn't hungry. But the doctor had found her slightly anemic and she'd lost weight, so he had been very insistent that she eat three meals a day, whether she was hungry or not, to keep up her nutrition.

The address he'd memorized from the medical record wasn't a familiar one, and for a moment he wondered if she—the donor—could have given a phony address. But he checked a local map and found the street—Hadley Road—on the outskirts of town.

How should he approach the situation? He'd never considered himself famous, but as a top crew chief in the NASCAR Sprint Cup Series, his picture had been in racing magazines from time to time and occasionally in the sports sections of newspapers, so he wasn't completely unknown, especially in the NASCAR world. More than once he'd been stopped in grocery stores or approached in restaurants by people who recognized him and wanted his autograph. After all these years, it surprised him that it still felt like a pat on the back. Even when the circumstances were inconvenient, he did his best to be affable. Trying to hide his identity in this situation, especially so close to home, therefore, probably wasn't a good idea. If this organ donor truly wanted to remain unknown, his showing up could put a jinx on her generosity. He couldn't afford to jeopardize what Kim needed so desperately.

Maybe he should watch the place for a while and hope to catch a glimpse of Nancy Jean Smith. Most likely he'd be wasting his time. Stakeouts were a professional investigator's job. He ought to call Rod Callison, the detective he'd hired, and let him handle the situation. But he didn't want to wait.

He would go to the address and ring the bell. If

a woman he didn't recognize answered the door, he'd say, "You're not Nancy Smith," give her a second to contradict him, apologize for bothering her and walk away. If she said she was, he'd say she wasn't the Nancy Smith he was looking for. There were probably hundreds…thousands of Nancy Smiths.

If it was Sylvie…

Hadley Road ran through a remote part of the city, an older section that hadn't yet come under gentrification. Number 743 never would. It was a two-story building with asphalt-shingle siding that was designed to resemble stone and brick. It hadn't fooled anyone in its heyday, and that had been a long time ago. Now it looked derelict. Apartment 203 was the second from the left on the upper floor.

Hugo parked his SUV at the curb close to that end of the building, rolled the windows up tight, in spite of the Indian-summer heat of October, and locked the doors. The concrete path that led from the cracked sidewalk was in equally poor repair. The steps up to the second-story balcony, however, were metal and reasonably new. They rang out as he mounted them, an unintended alarm for residents of people arriving.

The red door to apartment 203 was metal and faded. Beside it was a bell button with a piece of tape over it, indicating it didn't work.

The butterflies in his stomach were taking on the dimensions and temperaments of bats on a rampage.

He knocked on the door. No immediate response. Not a sound. Maybe the occupant wasn't home. He knocked again. This time he thought he heard movement inside.

He waited, then knocked a third time.

Finally the door opened.

CHAPTER TWO

THE WOMAN STANDING in front of him had a world-weary look. Limp brown hair, generously streaked with gray, hung to her shoulders, unadorned, uncurled, neglected. She was slender, almost skinny, and the plain cotton shirt and baggy jeans she wore didn't do much to enhance her appearance.

But there was no question who she was.

Sylvie.

Her amber-brown eyes, in spite of the crow's-feet subtly radiating from their corners, were still startlingly vibrant.

The two middle-aged people stared at each other. It took several moments for him to realize that although she wasn't pleased to see him, she wasn't surprised, either.

He finally managed to swallow. When at last he spoke, it was to say just one word. "Why?"

Why did you leave me? What am I going to do now

that you've been found? Do I tell Kim? What will her reaction be?

"Hello, Hugo," she said quietly.

Only two words, but he instantly recognized the voice, its gentleness. It shocked him that he could still hear the damaged young girl he'd met selling souvenirs for a vendor at the Charlotte race track all those years ago. If he closed his eyes all that time would disappear.... But he couldn't close his eyes. And three lonely decades couldn't be made to go away.

It wasn't a smile that twisted the corners of her mouth, but something did. Something familiar. "Come inside." She swung the door wide and backed up, giving him space to move past her.

He stepped across the threshold, stood only far enough inside for her to close the door behind him. The room was dim and shadowy, lit only by the spotlight focused on a quilting frame in the far corner to his left. The rest of the space seemed used and shabby, not at all cozy.

"Sit down," she invited, circling him and gesturing vaguely toward a sagging couch and pair of easy chairs. No rings on any of her fingers, he noted. "You still drink iced tea by the gallon?" she asked. "I have some in the ice box. I'll get us both a glass."

He hadn't heard anyone call a refrigerator an ice box in years. She went to the utility-size kitchen on his right. A counter with a post at the open end separated it from the living room. He drifted to one of the two scarred wooden stools there and half sat on it, his elbows propped on the worn Formica top.

He couldn't take his eyes off her as she leaned into the refrigerator. At nearly fifty, she still had the shape of a much younger woman. She'd always been slender, at least during the time he'd known her. Gazing at her now, he doubted she'd put on five pounds since the last time he'd seen her. She turned around, holding a half-gallon jar. Swinging her hip to close the door, she placed the glass jar on the work surface just below the high counter.

"How did you find me?" she asked without making eye contact with him.

Again he was struck by the lack of anger, or any other real emotion, in her question.

"Nobody told me," he said, "if that's what you're asking. Nobody snitched. I stole a peek at a medical form when no one was looking."

She merely nodded, taking the information in stride. "I'm sorry I don't have any mint for your tea. You always liked mint," she said. "I do have lemon, though." Still avoiding eye contact, she spun around again, reached up and removed two tall glasses from an overhead cabinet. From what he could see, the stored contents were minimal. This was a place

where one stayed temporarily, he realized, not a
home where one lived. Where was home? he
wondered. What was it like? Was anyone there
waiting for her?

He tried not to stare, but he couldn't help himself
as she went about the task of removing ice trays from
the small freezer compartment of the ancient fridge.
Her movements seemed self-conscious as she
dropped the cubes into the glasses, filled them with
cold tea without spilling a drop, returned the jar to
the fridge and removed a small plastic bag contain-
ing already-cut wedges of lemon.

Neither of them said anything during this process.
She had to be nervous—he certainly was—but she
performed each task with deliberate care. She posi-
tioned an open two-pound sack of sugar on the
counter and gave them each cheap, long-handled
iced-tea spoons from a drawer. Having finally run out
of things to do, she picked up her sweaty glass, leaned
against the small stretch of counter between the refrigerator and stove and gazed expectantly at him.

"Why?" he repeated.

"Why what?" she asked, then paused thoughtfully.
"I think a better question would be where to begin."

"Why did you run away?" He tried not to sound
accusatory, but he supposed it was impossible.

She shook her head and crooked an ironic, sad

smile. "Oh, Hugo, that wasn't the beginning. That was the end."

Not the response he'd expected. "I don't understand, Sylvie."

"How's Kim?" she asked, ignoring his statement.

"Coping. She has a chance to live now, thanks to you."

"I would happily give my life for her."

He didn't doubt it. Somehow he'd never doubted that she loved her daughter.

"Then why did you leave?" he asked. "Why did you abandon her? How could you walk away and leave a four-year-old child behind?"

In the reflected light of the sewing lamp he saw his former wife the way she'd been the first time he'd set eyes on her. The melancholy that enveloped her. It was at the Charlotte track the afternoon before the season's first race there....

Hugo's older brother, Troy, had been driving short track for several years and, contrary to his personal hype, had done only moderately well. Good-looking, charismatic and popular, he'd nevertheless managed to snag a sponsor in the NASCAR Nationwide Series for one season. Unfortunately he hadn't lived up to his own bluster there, either, and the sponsor had declined to bankroll him for another season, so Troy had wrangled a job as a crew chief for one of his buddies—temporarily, of course, until he was able to corral another sponsor. He'd also hired his kid brother as a catch can man, the member of the pit crew who held a special container to catch any overflow when the car was being refueled. It was important to make sure there was no spillage that could catch fire when the car burned rubber pulling out of the pit. The work was relatively easy, the pay decent. Best of all, they were part of the NASCAR racing world.

Hugo had had a few hours off that afternoon, and being a nineteen-year-old single guy, he'd decided to check out the action among the fans. Like his macho big brother, he'd never had much trouble finding female companionship, and, wearing the team uniform, he pretty much had his choice among the willing.

Then he saw this young gal selling souvenirs out of the back of a trailer. She wasn't dressed to draw attention to herself like some hawkers were. No skintight jeans or fringed leather cowgirl getup. She wasn't even wearing makeup, as far as he could tell, but she sure was pretty. He passed by the concession several times, not quite sure why he was so interested. Quiet, unassuming, even shy, she really wasn't his type, but there was something about her that intrigued him, a kind of little-girl sadness. When a race fan who'd had too many beers starting giving her a hard time about the price of something, it brought out Hugo's protective instincts. He'd intervened on her behalf. The pushing match that followed didn't quite rise to the level of a fistfight, but it came close. More important, it gave him the opportunity to meet Sylvie Ketchum.

She thanked him in a strong southern accent that made him smile, but then she turned away, as if to dismiss him. She wasn't impressed by his well-toned body or his gallantry, or even by the fact that he was a member of a racing team. Undiscouraged, even tantalized by the challenge, Hugo asked her for a date.

She shot him down that day and the next, but he managed to catch up with her late Sunday afternoon when she was helping the concession owner pack up after the race. It turned out she wasn't the man's daughter, as Hugo had assumed, just locally hired help, and to his utter shock she was going to walk the mile and a half to her home. He got his pickup and offered her a lift.

She balked, as he somehow knew she would, but again he persisted. She eventually relented when her boss assured her he knew who Hugo was and promised to identify him to the police if anything happened to her.

That afternoon was when he found out about her three-year-old daughter, a perfect little pink-cheeked girl who clearly adored her mama and was treasured in return. Sylvie had probably expected him to be discouraged by her having a child, but he wasn't, not when he learned there was no Mr. Ketchum.

So many years ago. Simpler times, or so they seemed in retrospect.

"So why did you leave?" he repeated now.

SYLVIE WENT THROUGH the motions of taking a sip of her tea, but her stomach was too upset for her to do more than wet her lips. She'd been dreading this meeting, done her best to avoid it. Yet it seemed to her she'd been trying to prepare for it since the day she'd packed a few meager belongings in a tiny knapsack, kissed her napping daughter goodbye and slipped out the back door, while the babysitter watched TV in the front room.

"I had no choice, Hugo," she answered defiantly. "Staying would have been worse."

He gaped at her, brows knitted. He wasn't satisfied with the answer. She couldn't expect him to be, not without further explanation, and she knew he would get it. He'd always been dogged. It was one of the things she'd admired about him, his quiet, non-threatening but unrelenting persistence. Clearly he hadn't changed. He wouldn't be here now, after all these years, if he was one to give up, to let things go.

Their first meeting was still clear in her memory.

She hadn't made many sales that day, though there had been plenty of foot traffic, and she was worried her boss might fire her. Hugo had passed by once, taken a brief glance at her and moved on, good-looking and a little cocky in his team uniform. Then he'd passed by again. This time he'd smiled at her. She did all she could do not to smile back. She'd had no intention of encouraging him or any other man. A few guys had made overtures, some less subtly than others, but she'd learned how to say no so that they understood it.

Hugo had been different. She hadn't been sure why, except that when he'd smiled at her, he hadn't made her feel like prey. It was a different sensation, as if he'd appreciated her for herself, not as an object or a means to something else, but as a person. That had been a new experience for her.

Observing him now, after thirty years, she realized his looks hadn't changed, not much, anyway. His face no longer had the fresh glow of a teenager. The cockiness had been superseded by maturity. The thick dark hair of his youth was cut shorter now, and there was a distinguished sprinkling of gray at the temples. The man of fifty was even more attractive than the boy of nineteen. Subtle worry lines etched the corners of his eyes, but their hazel-greenness was as intense as it had been back then.

The next minutes and hours were going to be difficult for both of them. When it was over he would hate her even more than he had when she'd walked away, yet she still felt safe with him. No other man had ever made her feel the way Hugo Murphy had. He would hate her from the depths of his being in a little while, but he would never hurt her.

She'd made a terrible choice leaving him, leaving Kim, but she knew now more than ever, standing so close to him, that it had been the *right* choice.

The question was whether he could ever forgive her.

CHAPTER THREE

SHE PULLED a napkin from a packet on the corner of the counter and handed it to Hugo to use as a coaster. Wrapping another around the base of her own tea glass, she circled the end of the counter and moved to one of the easy chairs, inviting Hugo to take a seat with the wave of her arm. He chose the couch, settling into its far corner, facing her.

A moment of reflection passed before he said, "I searched high and low for you, Sylvie. Where did you disappear to? I even hired private detectives. They were eventually able to find your family, but your folks claimed they hadn't seen you."

She almost laughed at the thought of their meeting. "You visited my family?"

"Up in the mountains. Yes."

She could picture in her mind exactly what he had seen. A ramshackle house that hadn't been whitewashed in years, a barn that never had been. Chickens running wild.

"Then you know why I wouldn't have gone back there," she said.

"They were plain country folks," he acknowledged, "but they were still family."

How polite he was being. Smiling sardonically, she said, "You don't know anything about life there. About them."

"No, because you would never talk about it."

As if talking about it would have done her any credit. Some things were best left unsaid. "Who did you see there?" she asked.

"Your parents. No one else would speak to me. They didn't seem real friendly toward outsiders."

She snickered. He was lucky he didn't get a rump full of buckshot. "What did my parents tell you?"

"Not much. When I explained that I was your husband, your father was surprised, said I was better off without you, that you'd probably run off with some other man."

It didn't surprise her, yet even after all these years it still stung. She'd vowed when she left that place she'd never let him hurt her again. For the most part she'd succeeded. "Did you believe him?"

"Of course not. I told him the idea was ridiculous, that you wouldn't do such a thing."

She couldn't imagine her father taking very kindly to an outsider coming in and telling him he didn't know what he was talking about, especially when it came to his own children.

"What did he say to that?" Sylvie asked.

"He scoffed, said Kim was born out of wedlock, so it was obvious what kind of girl you were."

Except, Sylvie reflected, he hadn't said it quite as politely as Hugo was recounting it now. "Did my parents tell you who the father was?"

"Claimed not to know."

"My mother, too?"

"I don't remember her saying much of anything."

No, she wouldn't have, not in the presence of her husband. If Hugo had found a way to talk to her mother alone, she might have opened up. Probably not, though. Outsiders were trouble, the enemy, not to be trusted. They left, and then you had to face your demons alone.

"Kim's father forced himself on me, Hugo," Sylvie said. She watched his reaction.

"What?" He stiffened, his eyes widening in shock. But he didn't question the truth of her statement. That gave her some satisfaction. "Who was he?" he demanded. Again she was consoled by the lack of a threat in his question.

"His name was Daryl Faykus, the son of my father's best friend."

"You never told me."

She could see he was shaken by the news. "Why would I, Hugo? Do you think I was proud of it?"

His brow was furrowed as he processed the information. "Did you turn him in?" he asked.

She huffed. "It wouldn't have done any good, I assure you." She could see that Hugo's initial response was to argue with her, maybe tell her she had a moral obligation to report it, but then he seemed to realize that in that environment, things were different.

"Did your family know?"

"I told Ma. She told me to keep my mouth shut about it."

"But why? Why wouldn't she want him to be punished?"

"Because by then Daryl was dead."

She watched a panoply of emotions cross her ex-husband's face. Bewilderment. Anger. Doubt. Was she making this all up? She had to admit that even to her own ears it sounded incredible. After all this time, it didn't seem possible—except she had lived it. She *knew*.

"I was fourteen," she said, "almost fifteen, when Daryl—he was seventeen—cornered me in the barn. It was the middle of the afternoon. My father and most of the other men were either out in the fields or in town or off somewhere doing chores. My mother had gone over to visit one of her sisters. No one was around. Daryl came on to me. I tried to fight him off, but he was a big, strapping farm boy. He was also drunk. He grabbed me in the barn and…I wasn't a willing participant in what followed, I assure you. When it was over, he told me he'd kill me if I said anything to anyone about it. I kept quiet because I believed him."

She took a breath, lifted the glass from the end table where she'd deposited it and was surprised to see that her hand was shaking. After all these years the memory of it…talking about it…made her want to cringe. She lowered the glass.

"A month later Daryl got himself stabbed to death in a fight. He was drunk again. It wasn't until a week after that I realized I was pregnant. I told Ma. She told Pa. He'd find out eventually, anyhow. It wasn't like I could hide something like that. He demanded to know who had done it. I didn't want to tell him because I knew what his reaction would be, but he threatened to beat it out of me if I didn't. I told him it was Daryl."

She looked away, not wanting to see the contempt and the pity in Hugo's eyes. "Telling him only made matters worse. He refused to believe that his best friend's son would have done such a thing, and he called me a few things for blaming a boy who could no longer defend himself. He wanted to throw me out of the house—"

"My God, Sylvie." Hugo ran his hand down his face and stared at her in shock.

"But my mother talked him into letting let me stay there at least long enough to have the baby. Afterward he let me continue to live with them, but the way everyone treated me... I couldn't let Kim grow up in that environment—marked, laughed at, called names. So I left and came to Charlotte."

"You told me your husband was killed in a car wreck."

She let out a mocking laugh and shook her head. "What did you expect me to say, Hugo? Tell you the truth? Tell you where my daughter really came from? Maybe I should have. Maybe then you would have left me alone, and all the things that happened later wouldn't have."

But by the time you came along, she thought, *I was starved for affection, for some assurance that I was better than the things I'd been called. You offered respect and I was grateful for it.*

"So what did I do that made you run away?" Hugo asked harshly.

She understood his anger, his disillusionment. She'd deceived him from the first, but at the time, she'd thought she was doing the right thing. It was an innocent lie, after all, a deceit that made no real difference in their relationship, and it protected Kim.

"Nothing, Hugo. The fault was mine, all mine. That's what I'm trying to tell you."

She watched him rein in his temper and admired his self-discipline. Other men might have lashed out with words and fists, but Hugo had never been that way. Of course, she hadn't told him the whole story yet, either. Maybe when she did...

"Nothing you've told me so far," he said, his voice tight but under control, "explains why you ran away, Sylvie, why you abandoned your own daughter. Do you have any idea what your leaving did to her?"

His words stabbed at her heart. Her sweet little girl. She fought to stay calm, to hold back the tears.

"I know," she said firmly, "that for all the pain Kim's endured, she's been better off with me gone."

He shook his head violently and bounded to his feet, turned from her, then turned back to stand over her. "For the life of me, I don't understand how you can say that." He glanced down at her. "You're her mother, for God's sake. You were her world. She loved you."

Sylvie lowered her head, twisted her fingers. *Loved,* he'd said, not *loves.* But then, why should Kim love her now? "And I have always loved her," she murmured. "I still do."

She remained seated while he began to pace the narrow space between the couch and the counter, his fists clenched. Back and forth, like a caged animal. All that was missing were the growls.

He finally lashed out. "What aren't you telling me, Sylvie?" He was standing over her again, hands in his pockets this time, as if he was afraid to let them loose. "We were happy together. You, me and Kim. At least I thought we were. What happened to change that?" He spread his hands. "Please help me understand, Sylvie. What the hell went wrong?"

"We were happy…" she admitted, almost wistfully, "…for a while. Happier than I had ever been before. Happier than I've ever been since."

"Then why did you leave?" he implored. He wanted to understand, but she wondered if he could after all this time. She wasn't sure she did herself.

"So much happened that year," she reminded him. "We got married. We settled down. Troy's wife had her second baby." *It was the best year of my life; it was the worst year.*

"Justin. Yes, of course I remember."

"A sweet, beautiful child. Then Ginny killed herself."

He bowed his head. He'd always been kind to Virginia. If more people had treated her the way he had…

"Do you know why she killed herself, Hugo?" she asked.

"I didn't at the time," he said, looking up, his eyes shiny. "She had a nice home, two happy children. It made no sense. But since then we've learned a lot about depression. Maybe that was it. She was always so quiet, so shy." He paused. "She had such a wonderful laugh. Do you remember it? Maybe she was manic-depressive or suffered from postpartum depression, I don't know."

"She had a right to be depressed. She had a toddler and a newborn. Troy brought drunken buddies home without notice and expected her to play hostess, dragged her to fancy parties with millionaires and celebrities, even wanted her to give interviews to journalists. She was overwhelmed, Hugo. Exhausted. It simply got to be too much. She was like me, a country girl, and all of a sudden she was in the middle of this high-profile, high-stakes life. Troy was quick enough to criticize and mock her when she made a mistake, but he never gave her any guidance so she could get things right. I sure wasn't any help. She got pregnant, got married, had Rachel, then got pregnant again, and all the time her husband was demanding more and more from her, at the same time he was chasing after every female under fifty." She shrugged. "It finally got to be too much."

Sylvie remembered the day it happened too well. Virginia had come to their trailer—no high-end motor homes in those days, just a second- or third-hand single-wide—and asked Sylvie to mind Justin and Rachel for a few hours. She said she needed to get some rest. She'd been up half the night with Justin, who'd been colicky, then Troy had come home at three in the morning, woken her up and wanted to have sex. Sylvie had taken one look at the exhausted girl and agreed to babysit for a while. Five hours later, when Virginia hadn't reappeared, Sylvie went with the kids to Virginia's trailer and found her dead, an empty bottle of sleeping pills on the nightstand.

"Did you know she was going to kill herself?" Hugo asked.

"Of course not. If I had... But I should have realized. I was going through some of the same problems myself, but I didn't have a young baby and an infant to take of. I should have helped her more. Maybe if I had... She died, and no one seemed to care."

"That's not true. You cared. I cared."

"Troy didn't. He was her husband, but he was more embarrassed by her suicide than heartbroken. His big concern was who was going to take care of the kids."

"It was a valid concern," Hugo argued, but without conviction.

"Yeah," she said fatalistically. "A valid concern.

But if you recall, after the funeral, he left the kids he said he was so worried about with us for the night so he could shack up with some bimbo—"

"He had a weakness—"

She let out an outraged snort, glared at him, got up and stalked to the kitchen area and refilled her tea glass. Hugo hadn't touched his.

"After all these years and all that's happened, you're still defending him," she jeered as she returned the jar to the refrigerator. Then she spun around and shook her head. "Amazing. Totally amazing."

"He was my brother, Syl—"

"And Daryl was the son of my father's best friend. So what? That didn't change what they did."

An expression of alarm filled Hugo's face. "What are you saying, Sylvie?" He paused, then gaped at her. "Surely you're not suggesting…"

"Poor Hugo." She went back to her seat, plopped down into it, her temper continuing to build in spite of her determination not to let it. She knew she had to maintain control, so she let a moment pass before speaking.

"For all your worldly success," she finally said, "you can still be so blind, so naive. Troy was a piece of…" She swallowed the last word, took a deep breath, willed her heartbeat to slow. "He came on to me, Hugo. When he did, all the old emotions, the overwhelming, sickening feelings of helplessness and humiliation I'd suffered with Daryl, came crashing down on me. Daryl robbed me of my innocence. Now Troy was telling me I still wasn't safe."

He stared at her. "I don't believe you."

She laughed bitterly, stared down at the stained carpet, then shook her head. A moment passed.

"That is precisely why I had to leave, Hugo," she said in a near whisper. "Because I knew you would never believe me. It would have been my word against his, and he was your sacred brother, the man you looked up to, though God only knows why. I was just the farmer's daughter you'd married."

"That's not fair."

If only this ache for you in my heart would go away. "Life isn't fair," she said. "Haven't you figured that out yet?"

He rose, refused to meet her eyes, paced. "When and where did this incident take place?"

At least he didn't say this *alleged* incident, though she couldn't help hearing it implied in his tone.

"About a week after Ginny died. It was during the day. I was minding the kids. As usual," she added sarcastically. "He stopped by supposedly to see how they were. It was their nap time."

Hugo listened without saying anything.

"They were all sleeping in the living room,

because it was easier for me to keep an eye on them there while I was ironing."

The layout had been a standard one. Living room at one end, bedroom at the other, with the kitchen and eating area in the middle.

"Troy asked me to get him a soft drink. I hoped he'd take it and leave, but when I went to the refrigerator to get it for him, he came up behind me, and he… He put his hands where they had no right to be. I jumped. He laughed and started to tell me about all the fun, all the good times we could have together. He was using some of the same words and vulgar expressions Daryl had used. No, no, I told myself, not again. Not again. I began to tremble, to cry. I begged him to go, to leave me alone. I was terrified, but all he did was smirk. He'd leave for now, he said, but he'd be back. He went to the door, put his hand on the knob, then turned around to face me. Smiling, he promised me if I ever as much as whispered a word about this to you or anyone else, I'd be sorry, sorrier than I'd ever been in my life. He'd make sure of it."

Hugo stared at her for a long moment. "You believed him?"

She snuffled. "Oh, yes, I believed him. I'd grown up with men exactly like him, Hugo. Cold, selfish bastards without consciences. You don't want to admit it, but you know it's true. When Troy didn't get his way, he could be vicious."

A tense minute elapsed in silence. Finally Hugo rose, took a step toward the quilting frame, retreated, faced her.

"He would never have done that. It's ridiculous. You're lying," Hugo whispered, but his averted eyes silently acknowledged the accuracy of what she'd said. "Wait." He peered at her. "This doesn't make sense. By the time you ran away, Troy was dead. He wasn't a threat to you anymore. So why did you really leave, Sylvie?"

She looked him full in the eyes without flinching. *The moment of truth.*

"Because I killed your brother."

CHAPTER FOUR

DEAD SILENCE. All movement stopped. Except for the beating of his heart.

Gradually Hugo became aware of the sound of traffic seeping in from the street outside, but it was as if he was hearing it echo through a long, dark tunnel.

He gazed at Sylvie and wasn't sure who he was seeing. She could have been a young girl or an old woman. Either way, she was a stranger.

I killed your brother.

His mind crept back to a rainy night in June.

He'd been battling the flu, had put in an especially hard day at the garage, had come home later than usual and gone immediately to bed, though the sun hadn't set yet. Hours later he was awakened by knocking on the trailer door. Sylvie was asleep beside him, her back turned, facing the wall. She seemed not to have heard the rapping, and for a moment he wasn't sure himself if it was real or something he had dreamed. Then he heard it again, an insistent pounding and a man's voice shouting his name.

He'd thrown on his robe, staggered to the living room and opened the door. A sheriff's deputy was standing there. He asked for permission to come inside. Dread gripped Hugo's stomach. Lawmen didn't bang on your door in the middle of the night to bring you good news. His first instinct was to protest his innocence. But of what? He hadn't done anything.

"What's wrong?" he asked as he guardedly allowed the deputy to cross the threshold.

A minute later he knew. His brother had been found on the side of the road not far from the tavern where he spent too many of his evenings. Troy was dead, the apparent victim of a hit-and-run.

Hugo's big brother, the man who'd been like a father to him ever since their parents had died in a car wreck ten years earlier, was no more.

Sylvie had come out of the bedroom by then, robe wound tightly around her, rubbing bloodshot eyes. At the news of Troy's death, she'd stared wide-eyed at Hugo, then burst into tears. They'd held each other in a desperate embrace. He'd felt her whole body shaking, as if she was heartbroken, beyond consolation. She kept repeating how sorry she was. Three days later they'd buried Troy, and in all that time Sylvie had rarely stopped crying.

She was wrong, Hugo reflected now. He hadn't been completely blind to his brother's faults, but he had overlooked a lot of them. She was right when she said Troy wasn't always a good man, but he'd had his tender side, too. He would have been a better man if he'd let it show more often.

"Tell me what happened," Hugo demanded of her now.

She edged to the quilting frame behind him, moving stiffly, as if she were afraid her knees would buckle. After a moment she took up a needle, examined it, looking grateful it was already threaded.

"I'd been downtown shopping earlier in the day," she said, "and had stopped by the post office to pick up our mail. Troy was there. He must have parked in back of the building, because his truck wasn't in front. If I'd known he was there, I wouldn't have gone inside. No one else was around. We were alone.

"He cornered me, tried to put his hands on me, and in my fear and anger I slapped him. It infuriated him. He grabbed my wrist, squeezed so hard he left a bruise and told me if I didn't wise up, he'd take it out on Kim. I was terrified. I'd learned a few things since my encounter with Daryl, so I wasn't all that worried about him hurting me there in the post office, but I couldn't take a chance on him hurting my little girl later. I fled. I needed desperately to talk to you about what had happened, but then you came home…" Her voice trailed off.

"I was unavailable to you when you needed me most," he murmured.

"It wasn't your fault, Hugo. I've never blamed you for that day. You were sick and you'd had a long day."

"Just tell me what happened," he ordered.

She took a frustrated breath. "I'd asked Molly Shay, who lived next door, if Kim could spend the night over at her place with her daughter, Karen. The girls were excited about the sleepover, but when you came home, you were so pale. All you wanted to do was hit the sack. I was disappointed, but when I watched you lie down and fall asleep almost instantly, I knew it would have to wait. Still, I was restless, so I decided to get the mail I hadn't gotten earlier."

She took up a square of fabric, set it in place and made her first stitch. "The sun sets late in the middle of June. It was twilight by then, and rainy. There wasn't a soul on the street. At least no one I saw. I pulled into the post-office parking lot, went in and retrieved the mail from our box. As I was coming out I saw a Grosso truck drive by. I couldn't see who was driving it, but a second later I heard the driver blow the horn and saw him swerve violently to avoid hitting someone who'd just come out of Clancy's Pub. I got into our truck, started the engine and went in the same direction. In my headlights, I could see the pedestrian was Troy."

She lowered her hands to her lap and gazed blindly at them, as if she were seeing another scene before her eyes. "He was staggering drunk, as usual. Instantly I thought about Kim, my precious four-year-old, and I thought about the cowardly threat this man had made against her earlier in the day. I decided this was a good time to put the fear of God in him, to let him know I wasn't going to allow him to hurt my little girl. The street was deserted, and there was Troy, standing in the rain in the middle of the road, shaking his fist at the truck that was fading into the rainy darkness."

Sylvie again took up her sewing, her expression a mask of determination. "As he started toward his own pickup, which was parked on the other side of the street, I aimed straight for him—I was just trying to scare him. I expected him to continue running toward his truck and take cover in front or behind it when he saw me coming at him. Instead, for some crazy reason he stopped directly in front of me. I felt a thump.

"I wasn't even sure I'd actually hit him. He might have just punched the side of the fender in anger. I'd seen him do it before. Oh, well, I thought, God takes care of fools and drunks, and Troy Murphy was both.

I checked the rearview mirror, didn't see him and kept going."

She sighed. "It wasn't until hours later, when the deputy came pounding on our door, that I realized what I'd done. I hadn't run him over, that much I knew, but he hadn't punched the fender, either. Without intending to, I'd struck him. He must have staggered out of my line of vision and fallen dead."

"But you didn't say anything." Hugo's voice was a dull monotone.

She canted her head to one side, raised her shoulders and let them fall. "Who would have believed it was an accident, nothing more than a scare prank gone bad?"

Hugo's jaw tightened. She made it sound as if she was talking about some trick-or-treat caper.

"Just like with Daryl, no one knew about what had happened between him and me," she continued. "But everybody—except you, it seemed—knew that I hated your brother. I was sorry I had killed him, but I couldn't honestly say I was sorry he was dead."

Her brutal honesty shocked him. Was this the demure girl he had married? But she wasn't a girl anymore, just as he wasn't the idealistic simpleton she'd accused him of being back then.

"And what would have happened to Kim if I had confessed?" she asked. "Troy was the local hero, a guy who'd just lost his wife and had two motherless babies to raise all by himself. If he got drunk once in a while, showed interest in another woman, well, he was a grieving man. I, on the other hand, would have gone to prison. Under those circumstances I couldn't expect you to keep Kim. She would have ended up in an orphanage or a foster home. If my family, by some miracle, had come forward to take her, her life wouldn't have been any better. Hugo, I had to protect her."

He gave a slight nod, a mute acknowledgment that what she said was probably true. "And your way of protecting your little girl was to abandon her?"

She flared. "I didn't abandon her," she insisted. "I left her with you."

He tried to understand the words, to appreciate the distinction, but he was having problems fitting it all together.

"I don't get it, Sylvie. No one had accused you of the hit-and-run. Word was that Dean Grosso had done it."

The feud between the Murphys and the Grossos reached back a generation earlier, when Hugo's father, Connor, a NASCAR driver, had beaten out Milo Grosso in the last race of the season and denied him the trophy. Milo, who was now in his nineties and still as full of piss and vinegar as ever, insisted Connor Murphy used a fuel additive in his last pit stop. Some time after the altercation, Connor's motorcycle ran off a mountain road and he was killed. A Grosso truck had been seen following him before the accident, but the police were never able to produce firm evidence that Milo was directly connected to the accident. When Troy was killed and a Grosso truck had again been seen in the neighborhood, the parallels between the two incidents were inescapable, except in this case everyone thought Milo's grandson was the culprit. Dean and Troy had their own serious issues between them.

"There was no proof against you, Sylvie," Hugo continued. "Things were quieting down. You were safe. Troy had been in the ground almost a month by the time you left."

She got up and walked to the window beside the door. The only thing visible through the dingy sheer curtain and beyond the balcony rail was the fading green foliage of a hickory tree.

"After Troy died you said we had to take in his kids," Sylvie reminded him.

"There was no one else. You were always so wonderful with them. What was I supposed to do?" he asked. "Put them in orphanages or foster homes? What did you expect?"

"You made the right decision, Hugo. I'm not questioning that. And I tried to go along. I did my best.

But it was no good. Every time I looked at them I remembered that I had killed their daddy. They were a constant torment, and I knew that with time I would break under the pressure."

It made sense in a perverse sort of way, he decided, and it explained something else, too. He recalled how distraught she'd been at the news of Troy's death. He tried to tell himself it was just her reaction to a sudden, violent death, that she'd get over it.

"So you ran away," he said, "and you never looked back."

She spun around and glared at him, color suffusing her face for the first time. "Never looked back?" she nearly shouted. "How dare you! All I've done for the past thirty years is look back. You have no idea how much I've regretted that day, the days that went before it and every day that's followed, how I've wished things had turned out differently, always knowing they couldn't."

She settled despondently into the easy chair she'd vacated earlier. "I haven't forgotten a moment of our life together, Hugo, or of my daughter's life. I've kept track of the two of you as best I could, but always at a distance. It wasn't all that difficult really. NASCAR is like a family. Everybody knows everybody else, or at least *about* everybody else. You all live in fish bowls. I didn't miss that, but I missed you, missed my daughter more than I can possibly tell you, but at least I had the satisfaction of knowing she was safe. That was the one consolation I was able to take from the mess I'd made of my life. My little girl was safe, safer than she would have been with a guilt-ridden, paranoid mother who was doomed to forever look over her shoulder."

It was a long speech for Sylvie, but Hugo had no doubt she meant every word of it.

Stunned, touched, experiencing an emotion for which he had no name, he climbed to his feet, took his glass—the ice had long since melted—to the sink behind the counter and poured it out. His hand was shaking. He didn't know what he was feeling, except that it wasn't pleasant, that it left him uneasy, confused, hurt, ashamed. He'd wanted answers; he'd gotten them. And now he wished he could put the genie back in the bottle. But of course, he couldn't.

He leaned over the sink, his hands splayed on the counter, for a long minute before asking, "What now, Sylvie? Now that you're back."

"I'm not back, Hugo. You have to understand that."

He spun around. "What do you mean? Of course you're back."

She shook her head and rose slowly, like an old woman, to her feet, but when she looked at him it was straight on, with determination.

"I'm not back in your life, Hugo, and I'm not back in Kim's. After the surgery I'm leaving and you'll never see me again."

CHAPTER FIVE

"NEVER SEE YOU AGAIN?" An old, familiar panic swamped him. He had every reason to resent this woman, to hate her for all the pain she'd already inflicted. Now she was announcing she was going to do it again, inflict still more pain! "You can't just pop into people's lives and then vanish. It's wrong, Sylvie."

"Let me remind you," she said slowly, "that I didn't seek you out. You sought me, even when it had to be clear to you that I didn't want to be found."

He could tell her that he hadn't come here looking for Sylvie Ketchum but for the generous donor of a vital organ that was going to save his daughter's life—her daughter's life. But there'd already been enough deception, enough lies. He'd really been looking for the woman he'd married, the woman who'd given him a daughter, albeit by another man, for thirty years. Nothing short of death would have stopped him.

"This is cruel, Sylvie!" he declared angrily, though he managed to keep his voice down. "It's cruel."

Except for a momentary, undoubtedly involuntary tightening of her lips, she appeared unmoved. He'd always admired her refusal to give way to emotional outbursts. He was only now beginning to appreciate what that stoicism had cost her, had cost them both. It wasn't because she didn't care, but because she absorbed her feelings deep inside her. Maybe if she'd opened up, told him what she was feeling, experiencing back then, things would have been different. But what was the point of blaming her now? She'd served thirty years for her silence. So had he. The time was past, gone. It couldn't be retrieved.

"It's the only thing I can do, Hugo," she said with seeming indifference. "The sole reason I came back was to give Kim a chance for a normal life. Once my part is done I have no reason to stay."

"But…" he started, then stopped when he saw her adamantly shaking her head.

"You can't tell me I would be welcome here, and I can't blame anyone for not wanting me around. I bring too much baggage, too much pain." She gazed at him, her expression pleading, not for sympathy, but for understanding. "Maybe I can change Kim's future. I hope so. But I can't change our past."

"You're giving her the gift of life a second time, Sylvie. A new beginning."

She smiled wanly and returned her attention to the

patchwork of fabrics in front of her. "It sounds so neat and appealing, doesn't it? But if I were to stay," she continued, "every time she looked at me she'd see the mother who'd abandoned her, and she would hate me all over again. I can't blame her. In fact, I'd agree with her. Every time we'd meet I'd see the accusation in her eyes, no matter how hard either of us tried to suppress it. Hatred from a distance is bearable, the pain tolerable. Sometimes it's even cathartic, but up close it unbalances and ultimately destroys us."

The words were spoken quietly, judiciously. Only the subtle tremor in her hands betrayed the depth of emotion they harbored. She was right, of course, and he wondered when the simple country girl he'd married had gained such wisdom. Or had it been there all along, and he'd never recognized it?

"So you'll run away again," he said more heatedly than he intended. Clearly he lacked her ability to detach himself from the anger and pain writhing within him.

She sighed deeply. "Oh, Hugo, do you really think I can ever escape the things I've done, that I'm unaware of what I've missed over the years, that I'm oblivious to the life I've lost? Do you honestly believe I didn't think about Kim on her first day in kindergarten, that I didn't picture her at her ballet lessons?" She smiled up at him. "Do you really think

I haven't imagined in my mind all the milestones in her life? Her first day at school, her first date. Her high school prom. I saw the announcement in the paper of her graduating from college at the top of her class in three years, going on to earn her master's degree in microbiology. You have every right to be proud of her, of her accomplishments, of who she is as a person. Her goodness comes from you, Hugo. I have no claim to any of it."

"You're her mother. Once she understands—"

Sylvie interrupted him with a shake of her head. "Some things are beyond comprehension, Hugo, no matter how valid we think the reasons for them may be."

"But you can't just leave without seeing her, without giving her a chance to…"

"To what, Hugo?" she returned irritably. "To love me?" She refocused on her quilt. "That's not going to happen. All the excuses, all the explanations in the world aren't going to make her love me. I know that, and deep in your heart you do, too. This is the best way, the only way."

"You're not giving her a chance," he argued. "You're underestimating her. I'm not saying it'll be easy—it won't be. Everything you've said is true, but you're overlooking two things."

She raised one eyebrow expectantly, yet doubtfully.

"You're still her mother," he insisted. "Regard-less of what happened in the past, you're still her mother. Nothing you've done, nothing she may feel toward you at the moment changes that. You'll always be her mother."

"Biology," Sylvie retorted flippantly. "She's a bi-ologist. She understands that."

"And the second reason," he persisted, "is that you're saving her life."

"I'm no hero, Hugo. Let's not make me out to be something I'm not. The time for pretending is over."

"There's nothing 'pretend' about giving up a kidney. You're putting your own health in jeopardy for her. You're risking your life—"

"Saint Sylvie," she scoffed. "No, I'm not doing anything any mother wouldn't do for her child, and you're forgetting one very important detail. I killed your brother, Hugo. I killed Troy, the father of Rachel and Justin."

It shocked him to realize that she was right, that he had forgotten, for the moment at least.

"If I were to acknowledge who I am and hang around," she went on, "people would want an expla-nation for why I left in the first place and why I stayed away so long. Unless I own up to the real reason I fled, confess what happened the night Troy was killed, I'd be lying. That's hardly the way to start a new relationship. Lies have a way of catching up with us and making matters worse."

"We don't have to tell them everything."

"Hiding the truth is just a lie tied up in a pretty silk ribbon, but a lie just the same. Once the truth came out, it wouldn't be long before the sheriff showed up with a warrant for my arrest. What I've already done to Kim and her cousins is bad enough. Do you really want to put them through the emotional hell and humiliation of seeing me charged with murder? How is that going to make their lives happier?" She shook her head. "No, there's only one thing for me to do, and you know it."

She jabbed her needle into the pincushion at the base of the quilting frame and rose from her seat. Facing the window a few feet away, she peered out into the green bows of a tall, spindly pine tree.

"I'm sorry you found me, Hugo," she said with a tremulous voice. "I knew there was a danger that you might, but I was hoping you wouldn't. Now that you have, now that you understand why I did what I did, I need you to promise me something. Promise me, if you care anything for Kim, for your niece and nephew, that you'll keep my presence here secret. I don't want to hurt anybody any more than I already have. I'm not asking this for me. What happens to me doesn't matter. It's for them." She turned and faced him, tears running down her cheeks. "Please, Hugo. I beg you. Let me go. Let the past go. Don't pursue me after I leave."

He did then what he hadn't been able to do in thirty years. He put his arms around her and hugged her. She hung there for a minute, crying softly, before she raised her hands and gently but firmly extracted herself from his embrace.

She turned away, her head bowed, and murmured, "I'm sorry. I thought I'd run out of tears years ago."

His cheeks, too, were wet. "You have my word that I won't say anything to them or anyone else, and that I won't go after you if you bolt again. But I need a promise from you in return."

"What?" she asked through a sniffle.

"That you won't run before the operation, before the transplant."

She faced him with a wry, tearful smile. "I haven't come this far to turn around now. This is my only hope for salvation, Hugo. I'm not going anywhere."

CHAPTER SIX

BY THE TIME Hugo left Sylvie's apartment, it was nearly sundown. He found it almost impossible to believe he had actually seen her. But he'd done more than see and hear her. He'd touched her. Those few seconds were indelibly engraved in his memory. A few seconds that changed everything.

Harlan Strom lived in a modest split-level house in a quiet suburb on the outskirts of Charlotte. He and Hugo had known each other since kindergarten. Their lives had gone in different directions over the years, but it was a mark of the nature of their friendship that whenever they got together, it was as if they'd never been apart.

Harlan was puttering with a Weed Eater in his driveway when Hugo pulled in and cut his engine.

"Good," Harlan said, without bothering to greet him. "You're here. You have a mechanical background. Maybe you can get this darned thing to work."

Hugo gazed at the device. "Collecting antiques now? Why don't you just buy a new one?"

"Humph. You sound like Catie." He studied the well-worn implement. "But you're probably both right." He put it aside. "I can't complain, really. Considering how many years I've had it, I guess I've gotten my money's worth."

He came across as a skinflint, which wasn't accurate at all. He could be extremely generous, as least as far as other people were concerned. For himself, however, he'd probably accept the title of "frugal" and wear it proudly.

"I have a six-pack here," Hugo announced, "that needs either consumption or refrigeration."

"I bet we can take care of both."

Harlan led his old friend through the two-car garage into the kitchen, which he admitted was grossly underused, handed Hugo one of the beers, withheld another for himself and put the remaining four in the refrigerator. They proceeded from there past an informal eating area through sliding-glass doors out onto a covered veranda beside a swimming pool. The day's sun was waning, but the color show it spread across the streamered sky was reflected in glistening patches on the smooth surface of the water.

They snapped the tops off their beers and settled into upholstered lawn chairs. Harlan's wife, Lynette, had died years earlier, leaving him with a young daughter. Raising her by himself gave him something in common with Hugo.

"How's business?" Hugo asked as they settled down. Harlan owned a construction company that had grown and prospered over the years. Not long ago he'd completed a total renovation of the house Rachel had inherited from her father.

"Can't complain, except that I have more work than I can handle."

"You did a great job on Troy's old place," Hugo remarked. "Rachel's very pleased."

"The house is small but sound, and the location on the lake perfect. Buying it when he did was a smart move on Troy's part. Bringing it into the twenty-first century was a fun challenge, and Rachel's got good taste. She knows what she wants. What's even more important from my perspective is that she didn't keep changing things every five minutes."

"The girl's got a mind of her own, that's for sure." This talk about Troy's house was as good a segue as any into the real purpose of his visit. They each took another sip of beer.

"How much do you remember about Troy?" Hugo asked casually.

Harlan looked at him curiously. "Your brother?" It was hard to recall the last time they'd discussed Troy, except to refer to him as the original owner of Rachel's house. "I remember you hero-worshipped him."

Hugo didn't deny it. "But what did *you* think of him?"

"Why are you asking, old buddy? He's been gone…what? Thirty years? Why dredge up those unhappy times? Seems to me they're best forgotten."

"Fixing up his old house," Hugo answered, hoping his lie was convincing, "has gotten me thinking about him. After all, he was my big brother." He paused. "Or maybe I'm just getting old."

"You better not be, friend, because if you are, then I am, too, and I'm not ready for a rocking chair."

Hugo laughed. Neither of them were ready for gliders on the porch, but they weren't young bucks anymore, either, as his body periodically reminded him. "So what did you think of him?" he asked, refusing to be distracted.

Harlan studied his beer can a moment before answering. "Well—" he hesitated "—now that you ask, I guess I owe you a straight answer. I didn't like him, Hugo. To be honest, I was afraid of him. I didn't trust him. I detested the way he treated people, especially women. I thought he was a real—"

Hugo's eyes widened. "I had no idea you felt that way," he said.

Harlan pursed his lips, as if he wasn't convinced

of the truth of the statement, but he didn't challenge it, at least not directly.

"He was good to you," Harlan said. "He treated you decently. It was one of the contradictions of his character that he was a good big brother to you, set high standards, expected you to do what was right, but he seemed to think he was exempt from the same rules. He liked to put people down, especially people he knew couldn't fight back. Do you remember Rufus, the old guy who cleaned up the garage, did the scud work? Your brother seemed to take special delight in humiliating him, when all the man was trying to do was earn an honest living to support his family. Troy knew Rufus could barely write his name, but he seemed to go out of his way to ask him to read him the instructions on a label, or he'd leave notes for him to do things, then bawl him out for not doing them. I hated that Rufus never fought back, that he didn't just up and coldcock your brother. I don't think anyone would have raised an eyebrow if he had, but Rufus was smart enough to know he couldn't win. Now that I think about it, I guess in the end Rufus did win. He outlived Troy by twenty-five years and brought up all his kids to make him proud. They're all successful professionals today."

Hugo hadn't thought about the old-timer in ages. "Could he have been the one who ran Troy down that night?" he asked.

Harlan pulled back, not even attempting to hide his shock at the notion. "You can't be serious. Rufus? If you recall, they checked him out. He wasn't even in the county at the time of your brother's death. Besides, Hugo, you know as well as I do that it wasn't something Rufus would do, and if he had, intentionally or by accident, he would have admitted it."

Hugo took a pensive swallow of beer. "Who do you think killed Troy?"

Harlan was clearly surprised by the question. "I honestly don't know. I can tell you this, though. It was someone who knew him. Maybe one of the women he used. More likely one of their husbands. I've never subscribed to the theory that it was an accident, even if it was a rainy night with lousy visibility. I think it was someone who hated or feared him, and there were plenty of those, male and female." Harlan stared at Hugo. "What's going on?"

Hugo shrugged and took another sip of his beer. "I guess it's just that with so much happening in our lives right now, I find myself getting nostalgic, wondering what might have been if things hadn't turned out the way they have."

His friend nodded. "It's a sucker's game, you know—playing what-if. We can learn from the past, but we can't change it."

Hadn't Sylvie said essentially the same thing?

"There's a lot of sorrow back there," Harlan continued. "Why don't you just leave it be? What's important now is the present and the future."

"I never realized you were such a philosopher," Hugo quipped, and raised his beer can in a salute.

Harlan chuckled. "My secret is out." A moment passed. "How's Kim?"

"Doing fine. It looks like we may have found a kidney donor."

Harlan's mouth fell open, then a broad grin spread across his face. "You old rascal, that's wonderful news. Why didn't you say something sooner? Congratulations! When will the operation be?"

"A week from tomorrow," Hugo said, pleased by his friend's enthusiasm and invigorated by it. "They need to run more tests, make sure all the compatibility issues are ironed out—"

"That's fantastic news," Harlan nearly shouted, then reined himself in. "She—and you—must be ecstatic. And a little scared."

"We all are, but it's her best chance. The doctors are hopeful for a complete recovery."

"Have you met the donor?"

"The person wants to remain anonymous." A true statement. "With the media…if word got out…"

If Harlan realized his question hadn't been

answered, he didn't show it. He merely nodded. "Understandable. No good deed goes unpunished."

"The main thing is that the blood type and Rh factor are the same—in this case, AB negative—though they'll run all sorts of other tests to make sure there are no other problems. I don't really understand them all."

Hugo got up and stood by the side of the pool, gazing into its turquoise depths.

"Kim will come through fine," Harlan assured him from his seat behind him. "She's strong, physically and emotionally, thanks to you, Wade, Justin and Rachel. You've brought her up right, my friend. Sylvie would be proud of you."

The statement caught Hugo off guard and sent an icicle slithering down his spine. It was their first mention of Sylvie, and his childhood friend was talking about her as if she was dead. But she wasn't. She was living in a shabby little apartment only a few miles away, sewing a quilt, waiting to give up a kidney for her daughter before again disappearing from their lives. He couldn't believe how much the idea of her leaving disturbed him.

He started to object, to correct his friend, then caught himself. "You think she's dead?"

Harlan upended his beer and placed the empty can on the glass-topped table at his elbow before answering. "I don't know, Hugo. It's the only explanation I can think of, because I can't imagine the woman I remember—a girl, really—ever leaving you and Kim the way she did. She loved you both too much."

"But how…?"

His host rose from his chair and came over to stand beside him, but he didn't say anything for a long time. "I don't know, but I've thought about it over the years. Sylvie was a sweet, gentle kid, had that kind of simple goodness we find so rarely. If Troy hadn't already been gone by the time she disappeared, I might have blamed him for her—"

"Troy?" Hugo snapped, then caught himself. He lowered his voice and smoothed his tone. "What are you talking about?"

Harlan smiled sadly, a little embarrassed. "You never saw the way he looked at her, and I often wondered why. I finally realized you just couldn't imagine your brother being so depraved that he would lust after his own brother's wife."

"You're wrong," Hugo retorted, incensed, shaken. Had he actually been that blind? Had everybody else seen what he'd refused to see? It didn't seem possible, but apparently it was true.

"I'm sorry," his friend said, and Hugo had no doubt he meant it. "I should have kept my big mouth shut. It was all so long ago, in another life. It's not important anymore. Forget I said anything. I shouldn't have."

He announced he was going to have another beer and invited Hugo to join him, but Hugo declined. "One's my limit. I'm driving," he reminded him.

"How about I put on a couple of steaks? Might as well use the fancy gas grill I've installed."

Hugo politely declined that invitation, too. He needed time alone. To think.

Trying not to show how spooked he felt, Hugo followed him to the kitchen. Harlan opened a second beer, sipped. They leaned against adjoining granite-topped counters and talked briefly about the upcoming race, about Justin's record to date and his chances of winning the NASCAR Sprint Cup Series championship. Harlan didn't go to away races, mostly because he didn't have the time, but he rarely missed the ones here in Charlotte.

Finally, on a light, bantering note about Hugo still having a full head of hair and Harlan being able to save money on haircuts—he had but a fringe left of what was once long and thick enough to tie into a ponytail—Hugo left his friend. He drove to his own house, a place that was so much bigger than the one he and Sylvie had shared for such a short time as husband and wife, a house much grander than the apartment where she now resided, a house in which he was utterly alone.

Sylvie was alive.

What she had told him, however, was surreal, incredible. Except…it all made sense. He had tried to reject her claim that Troy had attempted to force himself on her. The trouble was that at gut level he'd believed her, and now Harlan had essentially confirmed it. The admission sickened him, made him feel not just like a fool but dirty and ashamed. He'd failed in his duty as a man, and the realization made him want to vomit. His brother had possessed so many admirable qualities. Troy was a good, even great mechanic, and though he hadn't made it as a race car driver, he'd been acknowledged as a darn good crew chief. He'd exuded a masculine charm that made women go limp, and a charisma that convinced men to follow his orders. A born leader. He'd taken on the role of parent unconditionally and without complaint after their parents died. He'd provided as best he could for his younger brother, protected him, insisted he do well in school, then prodded him later to stand up for himself—like a man.

But Hugo couldn't deny that his big brother had vices, too, serious character flaws that in the end wiped out the virtues. One of them was, as Harlan had said, the way he treated women. Troy had done the honorable thing by Virginia after he'd gotten her pregnant, but he'd never treated her the way Hugo felt she'd deserved; he'd never treated her like a lady. It was true that Ginny, only seventeen when Rachel was born, wasn't sophisticated or well educated. But she hadn't been stupid or lazy, either, and for the short time she'd been a mother, she'd been a good one—patient, caring and protective. That she would kill herself, leaving behind two children under the age of two, had shocked everyone. Only decades later did Hugo begin to understand that it might have been postpartum depression. Nobody even knew the term back then. Undoubtedly it was that overwhelming sense of despair and helplessness that had finally driven her to take her own life. Two young children, one a newborn, and a husband who did nothing to lighten her load and who was no doubt sexually demanding at the same time he was being notoriously unfaithful.

That Troy had made a move on Sylvie had come as a complete shock to Hugo, not only for the contempt it showed for Sylvie, but for the disrespect it showed to Hugo, as well. Looking back now, he realized he should have been more watchful and protective of his wife. He'd been blinded by what he wanted his brother to be, at the expense of honestly seeing him for what he was, what he knew him to be.

Now he was in a new bind. What to do about Sylvie? What he owed her went far beyond words.

As a single mother and a victim of abuse, she'd come to him reluctantly. She'd placed her trust and vulnerability in his hands, and he'd failed her. She was right about how she would be received now by both her daughter and by her daughter's cousins, who were as close as siblings. Projecting Sylvie into the spotlight would only open old, painful wounds. But might it not also help heal them? Didn't Kim deserve to know that her mother was still alive, that she'd had good reason for leaving and that despite appearances Sylvie still loved her? Didn't Kim deserve closure, something she would never get without the two of them meeting face-to-face?

Hugo slept little that night and got up wearily on Tuesday morning to face another day, no more confident in how he should deal with Sylvie's return than he'd been the night before. But he had reached a decision. Now he had to implement it.

CHAPTER SEVEN

SYLVIE WATCHED Hugo leave her apartment, heard his SUV start up, listened to its distinctive hum blend into the sound of street traffic until it faded away.

He'd held her in his arms, and in that small capsule of time she could believe she belonged there. For that precious moment the nights of loneliness, the years of emptiness and despair had disappeared.

Now they were back.

No man had ever tempted her—except Hugo Murphy. In the years of her odyssey, she'd shunned male companionship altogether. She'd seen enough, experienced too much of the wrong side of men. Hugo alone had been able to make her feel like a person, not an object. He also made her feel like a woman. She'd gloried in that realization once he'd awakened it.

Now he was back in her life. The circumstances didn't matter. She and Hugo were, one way or another, together again, and that scared her.

He scared her. She genuinely feared him.

Not in the physical sense. Never in the physical sense. Hugo had never touched her in anger, never abused her verbally. But the way she felt when he did put his hands on her, when he ran his fingers over her skin, when he pressed his body against hers, was overwhelming her. She felt secure from the world, from other people, when she was with him, but she was powerless to protect herself against him, to safeguard herself from that warm, silky desire to be possessed by him. All she could do was leave.

If, on the day she'd kissed her daughter goodbye and walked out, she'd waited for him to come home so she could kiss him goodbye, as well, she would never have had the strength to leave. Instead, she'd slunk away in the light of day like a victim, the victim she had always been. She was stronger now, stronger and smarter. The years of loneliness had taught her courage, that she could handle whatever came her way. She would do what needed to be done—not out of fear, but because it was the right thing to do. She wasn't escaping this time; she was meeting a challenge and going forward.

Hugo wasn't perfect; he had his blind spots, but he was a good man, and she had been unworthy of him. She still was.

She had no choice. She'd have to leave him again,

disappear. She'd prepared for this contingency. She had a new identity ready. Transferring her modest financial assets wouldn't be difficult, nor would it draw anyone's attention. She would slip into another forest, content to let the birds consume the tiny crumbs of regret she would strew in her trail. He wouldn't find her.

She collapsed onto the sagging couch, rested her head against the warm upholstery and closed her eyes. It had been hard leaving the first time, torture saying goodbye to her sleeping daughter, but wittingly or not, she'd had hope ahead of her. Hope that somehow things might be made right, hope that someday she would be able to come back, that the sins of her past might be forgiven and forgotten. She'd been naive, of course, but wasn't all hope naive?

This time would be different. The years, for one thing. She wasn't a raw nineteen-year-old anymore with the prospect of half a century stretching out before her. She was a mature woman now with no illusions that most of her life still lay ahead, no dreams of deliverance. There would be no going back this time, no idealistic fantasy of reconciliation and reunion.

The little girl was all grown up and didn't need a mother anymore.

Tears dribbled down Sylvie's cheeks. No use

wiping them away. There'd be more. She thought of Hugo and knew there would always be more.

AS HE TOOK the turnoff onto Race Track Road and pulled into the parking lot of Fulcrum Racing, Hugo reflected on the adage that timing was everything. In this case, it certainly wasn't working in his favor. If the race this coming weekend were here at Charlotte, it would be easy enough for him to delegate some of the tasks as he'd done in the past, and slip away periodically to spend a few minutes or hours with Kim or Sylvie. But Martinsville was two and a half hours away by road, not counting the mega-traffic jams that surrounded every track on race weekends.

Rachel accosted him the minute he entered his office. "Where've you been? I've been trying to reach you."

His first thought was that something terrible had happened, but the casual, unaffected way in which everyone else seemed to be going about their business belied that. Whatever was bothering his niece was personal, but it had to be important for her to speak to him so brusquely. He reached for his cell phone.

"Oops. Forgot to turn it on."

Cell phones in their various configurations were wonderful devices, in some cases lifesavers, but to him they were also monumental irritants. He powered it up and found he had indeed missed three calls, all of them from her within the past hour.

"What's up?"

"We have a parts problem," she said. "The valves and rings I ordered before we went to Talladega still haven't arrived."

"Are we down for parts?"

"Of course not," she replied, as if the very suggestion was a personal affront. She was a good planner, well organized and able to anticipate problems before they became crises. He supposed at the moment she was nearly as stressed out as he was. The Chase for the NASCAR Sprint Cup did that. She was utterly professional as an engine builder, which also made her just a bit compulsive and at times impatient, especially when her brother's racing future was at stake. Kim's upcoming surgery only added to her anxiety. The two women had grown up like sisters and were very close.

"What's the problem, then?" he asked.

"You want spare parts on hand at the track in Martinsville on Sunday, don't you?" Being smart-mouthed with him wasn't her usual style. He took a deep breath.

"Rachel, this is Tuesday. If they don't show up by noon, call the company and light a fire under them. It's not like this has never happened before or that we don't have other suppliers."

She started to say something, but at that moment her cell phone rang. He watched her detach it from her waistband, snap it open and put it to her ear.

Within a second her features softened and she turned her back on him, then slowly wandered away toward the window. No need to ask who was calling. Peyton Reese, her husband.

Hugo smiled. Newlyweds. They'd married in August, but it was clear that a couple of months weren't enough to tarnish the glow. He hoped that glow never dimmed. He'd thought the same about him and Sylvie—until the day she disappeared without a word. He huffed quietly. No sense thinking about that now. He had other things to do.

He moved behind his desk and fingered his way through the stack of correspondence the reception-ist had left there. Nothing unexpected or urgent. He disposed of three of them summarily, chucking them in the wastebasket behind him, all the time trying not to pay any attention to the silly romantic sounds his normally sensible niece was making a few feet away. He was scribbling notes to himself for the upcoming weekend when Rachel made one final kissing sound and clicked the cell shut. She kept her back to him for a moment before turning around.

"That was Peyton," she announced.

"I hope so." He winked. "Everything all right?"

"Fine," she said with a tiny smile of smug satisfaction.

Hugo was still marveling at the "girlie" part of his niece that her husband had awakened when she started punching numbers on her cell. He had no difficulty overhearing her side of the conversation this time. Using language that was definitely more in touch with her gearhead persona, she began demanding immediate delivery of the missing components and insisting the distributor pick up the tab for the special shipping, if he intended to continue doing business with Fulcrum Motors.

Hugo was impressed, and the satisfied look on her face as she disconnected attested to her success in browbeating the poor guy on the other end.

"They'll be here in two hours," she announced as she sat back.

"That's good news," Hugo said offhandedly. "It's nice to know customer satisfaction is still a high priority. Oh, I almost forgot to tell you. Rogers has approved the new dyno."

Rachel had been lobbying for months for a new dynamometer, a million-dollar piece of equipment used to measure an engine's power output, insisting that the latest models had features their present one lacked. Dixon Rogers, the owner of Fulcrum Motors, had been dragging his feet on the request, claiming the company couldn't afford it. Rachel's response had been predictable. They couldn't afford *not* to get a new one.

Her eyes lit up and a big smile swept across her face. "He did? That's great. Now I can start working on him to upgrade our software."

Hugo laughed in spite of himself. How many females got turned on by a new piece of automotive test equipment? "I wouldn't start the new campaign right away." Rogers had a justified reputation for being tightfisted. "Give him a few weeks to get over this expenditure first."

She snickered. "Got it."

"Is Justin around?"

She nodded. "In fabrication, I think. He wanted to talk to Carlyle about some design changes. What's up?"

"I'll tell you later." He picked up the phone and started dialing, essentially dismissing her.

CHAPTER EIGHT

JUSTIN STEPPED into his uncle's small office wearing jeans, a team T-shirt and baseball cap. "You wanted to see me?"

Hugo had noted on more than one occasion how much his nephew resembled his late father, but he was even more aware of it today. Not quite as chunky as Troy had been, but then, back in the old days, being in shape and looking in shape hadn't been as important for the NASCAR image as it was now. Besides, Troy had been too lazy to work at keeping fit and too vain to think he needed to. His drinking hadn't helped.

"There's something I want to talk to you about." He waited until Justin had settled into the chair across from him before going on. "I'm concerned about Kim. Her transplant operation is coming up. The doctor's still running tests, but he says she's anemic."

Justin shrugged. "She told Rachel and me that he said it's not serious, that there's really nothing to worry about. Was she holding back, not telling us everything?"

"No, no," Hugo protested. "It's just that I worry."

Justin visibly relaxed, then lowered his head and nodded. "Yeah, me, too. But—"

"With her surgery only a week away, I don't want to take any chances of her not eating right or following the doctor's orders."

Justin looked at him askance. "I'm sure she's learned her lesson, Uncle Hugo."

The episode at the track that Sunday, like the one in Kansas a month ago, had been the result of dehydration. It was a serious challenge for people on peritoneal dialysis, because they had to limit the quantity of liquids they took in.

"Kim is a smart girl," Justin continued. "Her collapsing like that was a fluke. She went too long without eating, and she hadn't taken in enough fluids. Stupid mistakes, sure, but easy to understand under the circumstances. It was an exciting race. I just wish I'd come in first, instead of eighth, for her, but you know how keyed up she gets at the track."

"That's just the point," Hugo said. "She's agreed not to go to Martinsville, but she has me worried nevertheless. I'm thinking of sitting out the race this weekend."

"To stay with Kim and monitor her diet?" Justin chuckled. "Come on, Uncle Hugo. It's a nice thought, but I don't think she'll appreciate having you hovering over her. Besides, if anyone's in a position to fill that role, it's Wade. He's her fiancé."

"She's my daughter," Hugo objected.

Justin got up and came around the desk to put his hand on Hugo's shoulder. It was an unusually intimate gesture. "Kim's going to be all right," he said. "The doctor wouldn't have released her from the hospital if he wasn't happy with her condition." He squeezed his uncle's shoulder. "And if I didn't think so, I'd be staying behind, too, and fighting you for a place at her bedside. She's as much a sister to me as Rachel."

Hugo reached up and patted his nephew's hand. "I guess you're right."

Justin returned to his seat. "You know I am."

That, of course, didn't solve Hugo's dilemma. He should never have agreed with Sylvie not to tell anyone of her return. He would keep his word, but he wanted to be able to keep an eye on Sylvie, too. She had promised not to leave until after the operation, and he believed her, or wanted to, but could he be sure? He felt he had to keep her in sight.

As if the matter were closed, Justin said, "We're heading into the last six races of the Chase. I have a fighting chance—better than a fighting chance—to win the championship. I'm worried about Kim, too, but you've told me yourself, worry doesn't do any good. The best diversion for both of us is racing. When we're at the track, everything else fades into the background and we focus on only one thing. That's when we're most alive." He had the enthusiasm of a zealot.

Hugo only nodded distractedly. What his nephew said was true, of course, for once he got to the track, heard the roar of engines, smelled hot asphalt and rubber, felt the ground vibrate under his feet, all else would be forgotten. But at the moment Hugo's mind was filled with thoughts of, not Kim, but Sylvie. He'd dated occasionally over the years but never seriously. The few women in his life had never been a preoccupation, just a pleasant diversion. It surprised him how much he wanted to spend more time with Sylvie. Yes, he wanted to ask her more questions, try to understand how they could have let their lives spin so out of control, but that was only part of it. Being with her made him feel…young and richly alive in a way he hadn't since she'd left. Thirty years and he still wanted to be with her.

"Is something wrong, Uncle Hugo?" Justin asked, breaking the silence that had sprung up between them. "Is something going on I don't know about?"

He knows, Hugo thought. *He's found out about Sylvie.* "Like what?"

"I don't know. Is Kim sicker than you've told us? Does she need more than just a kidney transplant? Is she going to die?"

Hugo felt as if the air had just been sucked out of his lungs. He'd wanted to reassure his nephew that he was taking care of his cousin. Instead, he'd misled him into believing she was terminally ill.

"No, no, of course not," he said, relieved that at least that much was true. "I'm sorry if I gave you that impression. No, Kim's fine. Dr. Peterson says the organ match is virtually perfect. He's absolutely confident she'll make a complete recovery. She'll have to take antirejection medication for the rest of her life, of course, and getting those meds adjusted so that she's comfortable with them and can handle the side effects may be difficult for a while, but she's going to be fine."

Justin blew out a breath. "You had me scared there for a minute."

"Sorry," Hugo repeated. "I'm having a little trouble concentrating today." He laughed to lighten the moment. "You may have noticed."

He wished he could start all over again, start so many things all over, beginning with keeping his eyes open thirty years ago and protecting the woman he loved.

Three minutes after Justin had gone, Rachel

knocked on the open door to Hugo's office, her expression anxious. "Is it true?" she asked. "Is Kim sicker than she's told us?"

Apparently Justin hadn't completely believed him. "No, it's not tr—"

"Justin said you don't want to go to Martinsville so you can stay with her."

Hugh sighed. "I was thinking of staying behind this weekend so I could spend more time with her, but Justin's right. She's a big girl. She can take care of herself, and I'd probably just drive us both crazy hovering over her when I should be at the track. Relax, honey. Everything's fine."

She slid into the seat she'd vacated half an hour earlier. "I hope you're right. This is so scary. I was thinking maybe *I* should stay with Kim, instead of going to Martinsville, make it a girls' weekend, but then Wade told me Kim's planning on coming to the track."

Hugo was on alert. "What? Yesterday at lunch she agreed to stay home. When did she change her mind?"

Rachel shrugged. "I don't know. Overnight, I guess. It shouldn't be a problem. She understands what she has to do, and Wade will be there. We all will." Rachel rose, clearly eager to get back to work now. "You're sure nothing else is going on with Kim? There are no other health issues?"

"She's fine, honey. I swear." He waved her needless concern aside. "Is Wade here?"

"Sure. Want to see him?"

"Ask him to come by when he has a minute, will you?" Actually he wanted to see him immediately, but he'd stirred up enough of a ruckus this morning. He didn't want to compound it by demanding his car chief's presence. Besides, if he knew Wade, the guy wouldn't waste any time showing up.

He was right. A polite tap a few minutes later had him looking up to see Wade Abraham standing in the doorway.

"You wanted to see me," he said.

"Come in." Hugo waved to the chair in front of his desk.

Wade took it and waited politely.

"I understand Kim is planning on coming to Martinsville this weekend. Yesterday at lunch she agreed to stay home."

Wade compressed his lips. "She changed her mind last night." He shrugged helplessly. "I tried to talk her out of it, Hugo, believe me. I reminded her what can happen when she gets too wound up, but she insisted she's in better control now, said she'd go crazy sitting at home by herself when everyone else was at the track."

That sounded like Kim. She loved going to

NASCAR races, especially when she could cheer her cousin on.

"She also pointed out," Wade went on, "that this will be her last race before her surgery. She doesn't know how long she'll be in the hospital or restricted from traveling once she gets out, but it's almost certain this will be her last chance to attend a race this season."

That was undoubtedly true, but still… "When was she planning on telling me this?" Hugo asked.

"I was going to come by a little later." Wade leaned back in his chair, trying not very successfully to assume a posture of ease. "I want to spend as much time with Kim at Martinsville as I possibly can, Hugo, which won't be much if I have to stand by as car chief. So I was going to ask you if I could take this weekend off. I've told Brad Hatcher that he might have to hold the fort. He's fine with it, and I know he'll do a good job."

Hugo could feel his temper rising. Kim was making a bad decision. Wade, by alerting his number-two man that he might have to take over, was colluding in it, and now Hugo was discovering that things were going on within his team he wasn't aware of.

"There's no way Kim is going to Martinsville," he stated unequivocally. "It's much too dangerous."

"I—"

"She needs to be home resting, building up her

strength. Her surgery is Tuesday. We…she can't take a chance of something happening—getting in an accident, getting overtired. You saw what happened at the last race. She overdid it and collapsed. She also passed out in Kansas."

Wade jumped in when Hugo paused to take a breath. "That's precisely why I need to spend time with her," he said, "to make sure she's careful." He softened his voice without stopping. "But she'll be miserable being away from the track, Hugo, especially now with Justin doing so well. Happiness is a great medicine. You know that, and nothing could possibly make her happier than to be able to put her arm around her cousin's shoulders in Victory Lane."

Try as he might, Hugo couldn't find a flaw in the logic or the argument. Kim *would* be much happier, much more relaxed, in spite of the excitement around her, if she were with the people she loved, sharing the sport she loved.

He remained silent for several moments. Nothing was working out the way he'd planned. He'd hoped to cut himself loose this weekend to spend time with Kim, make sure she was getting enough rest and nourishment. He also wanted to keep an eye on Sylvie, but he seemed to be stymied at every turn.

"I'm counting on you to take good care of our girl, Wade."

Wade closed his eyes briefly and nodded. "You know I will."

Hugo rose and extended his hand. "It'll make things a lot easier for me this weekend knowing you're with her."

After his prospective son-in-law left, Hugo settled into his chair. If Muhammad wouldn't come to the mountain, the mountain would have to come to Muhammad.

CHAPTER NINE

TWO HOURS LATER, having put the finishing touches on the next day's travel plans for the team and for himself, Hugo pulled out of the Fulcrum Motors garage and drove directly to Sylvie's place. For years he'd tried to anticipate what would happen when he finally found his ex-wife. Now he had, and his reactions were completely different from what he'd expected.

He was angry with her, yes, but he'd expected that and was unapologetic about the resentment he felt, because he was convinced he had a right to it. For three decades he'd asked himself what he'd done to drive her away, all the time secretly believing he'd done nothing blameworthy, that he, like Kim, was the innocent victim of Sylvie's abandonment. What he hadn't bargained for was the overwhelming sense of guilt that swamped him now that she'd told him what had actually happened. He'd failed to protect her. What greater responsibility did a man have to the woman he loved than to safeguard her physically? It was bad enough that he was so invested in his own little realm that he failed to appreciate the problems Sylvie was facing in trying to adjust to a world that was completely foreign to her experience, that he was imposing responsibilities on her without asking the cost. But that he had failed to recognize the threat from his own brother was even worse.

When she answered the door, she didn't look any more pleased to see him today than she had the first time, but at least she was still there. She hadn't bolted. Not because of him, he knew, but because of Kim. Her daughter needed her for life—literally. Sylvie wasn't going to run away this time.

"You should have told me about Troy accosting you," Hugo declared emphatically after she'd let him in and closed the door behind him. Saying it, admitting that his brother was abusive, opened the floodgates of his outrage. He was angry at Troy, angry at Sylvie, but mostly he was furious with himself for being so blind, so stupidly foolish. He'd married a beautiful, sensitive woman, then taken her for granted.

She ignored the statement and proceeded to her tiny kitchen. "Have you eaten?"

Only when she mentioned food did he become fully aware of the aroma filling the room. Boiled beef, if he wasn't mistaken. Sylvie hadn't been a fancy cook. No gourmet sauces or delicate soufflés, but her down-home cooking had been to die for. Involuntarily he sniffed the air and was disappointed when he didn't detect the tantalizing fragrance of one of her cobblers. No one baked a cobbler—apple, peach, cherry, wild huckleberry—like Sylvie. The memory alone was enough to make his mouth water.

"I'm not hungry." At least he hadn't been when he arrived.

"Too bad," she said with a hint of humor. "I bought fresh horseradish to go with the beef, too." She didn't renew her offer. "Coffee?"

"Yeah, thanks." He parked himself on a stool. "You should have told me about Troy," he repeated. "It wasn't right to hold back something that important and then blame me for not knowing about it."

She filled mugs for each of them, left his on the counter at his elbow and took hers over to her chair by the quilting frame. She waited until he brought his to the nearby easy chair and sat down.

"There were a lot of reasons why I didn't, Hugo. Maybe you've forgotten how far society has come in the past thirty years, but I haven't." He waited while she threaded a needle, then jammed a thimble onto her right ring finger. "Like I told you last time, when my father found out I was pregnant, he cursed me." She lined up a square of blue cloth beside a matching one of red. "As far as he was concerned getting pregnant was my fault."

"Didn't you explain that you'd been—" he didn't want to say the word he'd been thinking "—coerced?"

She drew her first stitch with meticulous care. "You don't understand. It didn't make any difference. Not only didn't he believe me when I told him Daryl had done it, he insisted that if a guy forced himself on me, it must have been because I teased him until he couldn't control himself any longer. Either way, it was my fault."

Hugo shook his head, horrified at the situation she'd been in, ashamed that she didn't feel she could trust him. "You could still have told me," he said.

She examined the stitches she had taken. "I had no reason to think you would react any differently."

The statement confounded him, wounded him. He couldn't believe she had put him on the same depraved level as her father. The very idea was insulting. "I thought you trusted me."

"You never hurt me, Hugo, but you had a blind spot when it came to Troy." Exactly what Harlan had said. She continued sewing. "I was sure that if I told you your brother had come on to me you would have taken his word against mine."

He started to object but caught himself and fell silent. The uncomfortable truth was that she was probably right. He'd idolized his big brother, and in the years since Troy's death he'd repeated the myth that he'd been such a great guy to Rachel and Justin so often it was doubtful he would ever have recognized Troy's shortcomings, were it not for Harlan's candor last evening. Even now he had to compel himself to accept the notion that Troy was capable of terrorizing a woman, much less his own brother's wife.

Hugo saw her glance over at him, and in that fleeting second they both knew her judgment had been accurate. A fresh wave of guilt assailed him.

"Then there was my own shame," she went on, letting him off the hook without dwelling on it. "When you're told often enough that you're the spawn of the devil, you begin to believe it. I kept asking myself if what had happened wasn't my fault, if maybe I hadn't somehow led him on without intending to, without re-alizing I was doing it. Your brother was a good-looking guy, and he knew it. I don't need to remind you that women adored him, literally threw themselves at him. And of course he ate it up. Why should he think I didn't feel the same way? He was conceited enough to believe every female was madly in love with him."

"Did you know he was playing around on Ginny?"

She laughed, but without humor. "Hugo, every-body knew it. You did, too. You just weren't willing to see it."

She was right on that score, as well. "I still wish you'd told me."

"You don't know how many times I wanted to, how many times I started to." She paused, took a few more stitches. "That night—the night I ran him down—all I ever intended to do was scare him, send him a message that I wasn't like the other women he knew, that I wouldn't let him threaten me or my daughter. Once he saw that, I figured I could go to you and explain what had happened, what he'd done, why I was afraid of him." She swiveled in her chair just enough to face him. "And I decided if you didn't believe me I could take Kim and leave without having to worry about either of you coming after me. I'd be destitute again, but I wasn't afraid of work. Kim and I would be all right, and I would be free."

"My God, Sylvie, if only I had realized—"

"But it went all wrong," she continued, ignoring him. "He zigged when I thought he was going to zag. Instead of continuing to run straight ahead as I'd expected, he stopped like a deer caught in the head-lights and reversed direction. I never intended to hit him, Hugo. I certainly didn't want to kill him. I hope you believe that. I just wanted him to leave me alone."

She poised her needle over the colorful fabric and tried to take another stitch, but her fingers were shaking. Jabbing the needle into the pincushion, she lowered her hands into her lap and hung her head.

"I hit him, Hugo," she said with a shaky voice. "I heard the sound as my fender struck him. Then he was gone, vanished from sight. I didn't know I had killed him. I hadn't been going that fast. I imagined I might at most have broken an arm or a leg. I knew legally I should stop, see how badly he was hurt, but I figured he could take care of himself." She picked up her needle again, her nerves seemingly under control. "I've often wondered what would have happened if I *had* stopped, if I might have been able to save his life."

Hugo shook his head vigorously. "You couldn't have," he said. "You know what the coroner said. Troy's blood-alcohol was nearly three times the legal limit for intoxication. Even if he wasn't staggering, with that amount of booze in his system, his judgment would have been seriously impaired, which explains his zigging when he should have zagged. Either from the impact of the truck hitting him or him hitting the ground, he died instantly. You can take consolation in knowing he didn't suffer."

"I certainly hope that's true, but it doesn't exonerate me," she replied. "It was wrong of me to act in violence against him. After all, wasn't that what he'd done to me, though in a different way? It was shameful of me not to stop, not to try to give assistance. Instead, I kept going. My only excuse is that I was scared, more scared than I'd ever been in my life, too scared to even go home to you right away. I drove around for over an hour, finally circling back to town. By then there were police cars everywhere. I knew there was nothing I could do, and that there was no way I could explain why I was out at that hour of the night when you were home sleeping alone in our bed."

Reaching for the coffee mug she'd placed on the sewing table beside the frame, she lifted it to her lips, then made a face when she realized it had grown cold. Taking up her needle and thread yet again, she resumed sewing with painstaking deliberation.

"I went home and crawled into bed beside you," she said. "You were asleep. I could feel the warmth radiating from you. My insides had turned to ice, and I wanted so much to hold you, to have you hold me. But I was afraid to touch you, afraid of waking you and having to tell you what I had done. So I lay there awake, shivering, staring at the wall. I was still awake when the sheriff's department came pounding on the door. I was certain Troy had told them I was the one who'd run him down. Instead, the deputy announced that your brother was dead. I didn't know what to do."

"I remember how shook up you were," Hugo

acknowledged, "practically hysterical, and I wondered why. It wasn't like you were close to Troy."

Hugo was ashamed to admit that for a while he'd even entertained the suspicion that there might have been something going on between them. He knew Troy was attractive to women, and Sylvie was a woman, a beautiful woman. How else could he explain her extreme emotional response to his death?

Now he knew. "The deputy asked you questions and your answers didn't make any sense."

She snickered. "For once my background worked in my favor. Nobody expected much from a stupid mountain girl."

"I never thought you were stupid," he told her. "Neither did anyone who knew you, but you were always so shy, so modest. It was one of your qualities that I found so endearing. Not many people got to know you."

"I was out of my element, Hugo. I could never be sure what I was supposed to say or do. I wanted to fit in—for your sake—but I didn't know how."

"Everybody liked you, Sylvie."

This time her laugh was filled with derision. "If you believe that, you were even blinder than I thought. The people in your world made fun of me, Hugo, just like they did Ginny. I was the constant butt of jokes. They ridiculed the way I talked, the way I dressed, the way I combed my hair. I was comic relief."

He bowed his head. "Maybe at first, Sylvie, but not for long—"

"The country bumpkin, always good for a laugh."

Listening to her now, he was astonished that she was still smarting from the mockery. But some insults cut so deeply they're difficult to forget, even for those who find it in their hearts to forgive the people who inflict them.

For the first time, too, he realized that her slow, country accent had melted into a soft, pleasant drawl that was more charming than rural, and that her choice of words was far more sophisticated than it once was.

"I'll be leaving tomorrow for Martinsville," he said. "Come to the race on Sunday."

"No." Her answer was delivered without a moment's hesitation and unbending.

"You used to enjoy the races." Should he tell her Kim would be there?

"I'll watch it on TV."

"Kim will be there." He saw her flinch, an involuntary and probably unwelcome twitching of muscles.

"I've got a ticket in one of the grandstands for you." He placed it on the corner of the end table.

She shook her head. "I'm not going anywhere near that track or any other."

He knew from her tone that pressing the issue would only alienate her. Better to drop the subject. Let the lure of seeing her daughter convince her to change her mind. She hadn't insisted he take the ticket back. He'd leave it, let it tempt her.

He watched her sew for several minutes. Back when they'd been married, she'd been a meticulous housekeeper. She'd taken pride in keeping their little trailer neat and clean, as if it were a palace. Later, after visiting the ramshackle farm on which she'd grown up, he realized it must have seemed like one to her.

"What have you been doing all these years?" he asked. "How have you earned a living, supported yourself?" If the surroundings were any indication, she hadn't done especially well. This wasn't a condo or a suite at the Hyatt Regency.

"I've managed," she said, making no effort to be more informative.

"Doing what?"

"Whatever I could."

"Why won't you tell me?"

She glared at him over her shoulder. "So you can track me down later? Where I live and what I do is none of your business, Hugo. It's my business and it's going to stay that way."

"Am I still the enemy, Sylvie?"

CHAPTER TEN

SHE PAUSED, considered. "You were never the enemy, Hugo."

But she had been afraid to trust him, even as her husband. His responses to the harsh reality she had told him about the other day suggested she had been right in not telling him about Troy, but now she knew better. Even back then he might not have wanted to believe her, but in the end he would have. Unfortunately, she'd only just figured that out. It was too late. Years too late.

"I must have been the enemy," he said, "or you would have trusted me with the truth."

"I couldn't trust anybody, Hugo, not even myself." She toyed with the handle of the coffee mug. "You asked where I've been, what I've been doing all these years," she reminded him. "I don't suppose telling you will make any difference now. You'll get one of your private eyes—" she snickered at the phrase "—to follow me when I leave here. It was easier to hide in the days before the Internet, before all the tracking devices our high-tech society has created to rob us of privacy."

He didn't comment, but he was listening. That pleased her. He wasn't going to bombard her with questions, at least until he'd given her a chance to tell her story. Even as a young man he'd been remarkably patient. She remembered how he'd coped with Kim when she was tired and irritable, when she cried nonstop with an ear infection. Sylvie's father and uncles would have lashed out to the point of violence. Hugo never had, even when he was exhausted.

She thought back to that afternoon, the day that had changed her life forever, even more than the death of Troy Murphy had.

"I kissed Kim goodbye, then I walked out to the main highway and hitchhiked south. I had no particular destination in mind at the time, except that wherever I went, I knew I had to remain hidden, in the shadows."

Her mouth was parched. She took a sip of the cold coffee.

"I considered going back to my family, but not for very long. I wouldn't be welcomed there. Even my mother wasn't likely to sympathize with the story I had to tell. Ma's loyalties were to her husband, not to her children. Daughters left, like I had. The circumstances weren't really important. What was important was that the men were always around and in command. My life there, if my father let me stay, would have been even more miserable than it had been before."

Hugo nodded. He'd met the man. He knew.

"Getting lost in a big city seemed my best bet. I figured it would be easier than trying to hide in a small town. The trip south was frightening. Some of the people I met were as sweet as Sunday-school teachers. Others, well…let's just say they asked for things I wasn't willing to give."

Hugo muttered something under his breath. Sylvie couldn't make out the words, but she understood the sentiment. She'd managed to ward the creeps off, but they didn't improve her opinion of men.

"I made it to Atlanta safely," she continued. "I've never liked cities. I hate big crowds, the congestion, the noise and chaos. Back then they terrified me. I went hungry the first three days I was in Atlanta. I didn't know what to do, where to go. I slept in hallways and dirty alleys. I was convinced my life was over."

"Did you ever think of coming home?" he asked.

"Of course I did, but then someone took pity on me and directed me to a shelter. The kind souls there didn't ask any questions. They fed me and helped me clean up, then found a part-time job for me, scrubbing pots in a restaurant."

"Oh, Sylvie."

"The work was grueling," she went on, "but I've never been afraid of hard work."

She saw Hugo bite his lower lip.

"One opportunity led to another," she said. "Cleaning houses, scrubbing floors, mending clothes. They were all poorly paid jobs, but they were also paid in cash with no records kept. I used a variety of names until I was able to save enough money to buy a fake ID. That brought legitimate employment, mostly waiting on tables, and better wages."

Hugo shook his head, as if he couldn't believe what he was hearing. She didn't doubt that he *did* believe it, however, or she wouldn't have continued.

"I was getting by, but I still hated the city. I maintained my privacy, made no friends, so I had no regrets when I moved on to other places, to smaller cities, large towns, wherever I could find work. I changed identities periodically, just in case you were looking for me."

"I was," he assured her. "I had detectives searching for you, but they couldn't find you. Anywhere."

She smiled. It was a compliment of sorts. She didn't tell him that she prayed sometimes, especially in the dark of the night, that he would find her. What would have happened if he had? She'd never know.

"I dreamed about you and Kim," she said. "I tried to picture her getting bigger, maturing."

Abject misery overwhelmed her when she thought about her little girl growing up without her. She came close to returning to Charlotte several times, too, in those early years, but she always convinced herself to go on.

"I moved west, worked for a few months in Alabama, Mississippi, Louisiana. Texas beckoned for a while, then New Mexico and Arizona. I understood the allure of golden California, but I didn't feel it. I was and still am at heart a mountain woman. I crave green hills and forests, rushing water, rain and snow, as well as sunshine. The Northwest offered me all that."

"And that's where you live now?"

"Yes." She let out a soft chuckle. He would have found her, anyway, she decided. There really wasn't any point in postponing the inevitable. But what she'd said still stood—she wasn't coming back here. They had no chance for a life together.

"Makes sense," he said. "Familiar territory, yet far away from the Appalachians, where you grew up."

She nodded, pleased that he understood. "I learned a few things over the years—that I could make a decent living cleaning other people's houses, that I could enjoy the company of friendly people without making friends and that there was demand for my handicraft skills."

"It sounds like a lonely life, Sylvie."

She shrugged. "I was content," she assured him.

The places where she'd lingered were like road signs on a journey—unimportant once they were passed—away from the place where she'd belonged, away from the people she loved. Regardless of time, place or activity, Kim and Hugo were never far from her thoughts. At a loom, a quilter's frame, doing needlepoint, knitting or crocheting, she couldn't help picturing her little girl growing up with her daddy. Without her.

"When you began to make a name for yourself in NASCAR," she told him, "I followed you in newspapers and magazines. Getting information about Kim was more difficult and haphazard, but I knew my daughter was safe. That was all that mattered."

He bowed his head, obviously gratified by her remarks but troubled by all she'd told him.

"Then came the Internet," she said brightly, "and a new world of information opened up. The lack of privacy I constantly complain about gave me a chance to follow you much more closely."

She studied the brooding man who had been her husband. "You accused me of never looking back. You're wrong, Hugo. As time went on I discovered I could never stop looking back."

CHAPTER ELEVEN

"ARE YOU GOING to be all right by yourself?" Hugo asked from the doorway of the spare bedroom in his motor home. He hadn't been happy about her coming to Martinsville, yet Kim was sure he was glad she was there.

"Dad, I'll be fine," she replied. "It's not like I've never done this before."

The love and concern she saw in his eyes moved her deeply. He'd been her rock through all her crises, whether it was deciding which school to choose from the scholarship offers she'd received, encouraging her to go into the growing field of stem-cell research or approving of the man she'd fallen in love with. Mostly he'd guided her through the loss of her mother—when his own heart was breaking—and more recently been a constant source of encouragement when she was diagnosed with acute kidney failure.

She knew she could always depend on him.

Kim sat in the leather recliner, slipped on her

sterile gloves—an important step in protecting herself against infection—inserted the catheter through the port in her abdomen just below her navel, opened the valve to start the gravity flow of fluids from the overhead IV bottle, then opened her book, a historical romance set in the eighteenth century. The hour-and-a-half-long process wasn't painful or even particularly uncomfortable. Mostly it was inconvenient and a constant reminder of the fragility of her health. At least she wouldn't have to endure this twice-daily ritual much longer.

She reached the bottom of the page and realized she had no idea what she'd read. Sighing, she slammed the book shut, put it aside, leaned back and closed her eyes.

For days the question had been running through her mind. Who was the kidney donor?

Dr. Peterson said the match was nearly perfect. As a scientist, Kim knew the odds. What was the likelihood of a person with AB-negative blood volunteering to give a kidney to a total stranger? And how likely was it that such a person would be a nearly perfect match to the recipient?

From the moment she was diagnosed with renal failure and told an organ transplant was recommended, Kim had thought about her mother. Everyone figured Sylvie was deceased. Kim herself had declared her dead years ago, but she'd never really believed it, and she knew Hugo didn't, either.

How many times had she asked her father why her mother had left? His answers never made much sense, but it had taken Kim years to understand that he wasn't holding back, he wasn't hiding anything. He just didn't know.

Was her mother crazy? Had she wandered off somewhere and forgotten her way back? As a kid Kim had pictured her mom as a sad homeless person, stopping people to ask them how she could get back home.

Rachel and Justin's mother had killed herself. Had Sylvie? Why? And if she had, why didn't they know about it?

Kim had been only four when her mother disappeared, so her memories of her were a little vague, but they were all pleasant, happy. She remembered clapping hands with her mom, singing songs with her. "Twinkle, Twinkle, Little Star." "The Itsy-Bitsy Spider." And there had been cookies and milk. Mommy had taught her how to twist the two halves of the chocolate cookies to separate them, then lick off the cream filling before dunking the cookie parts in the milk.

She remembered waking up in the morning and from her naps in the afternoon and wondering if Mommy had come home yet. For years her last prayer every night had been, "I'm sorry, Mommy.

Whatever I did wrong, I'm sorry. I won't do it again. Please come home."

Days went by. Then weeks. Months. Hugo gave her a party for her fifth birthday, but it wasn't any fun. Christmas came and went.

School started. Years went by. But her mom didn't come home.

Was she back now? If she was, why hadn't she come to see her? If they did meet, what would they say to each other?

Kim had told Hugo she hoped the donor wasn't her mother. Because it would be easier if she wasn't. But what about getting answers? Didn't she want answers? Didn't she want her mom back?

Mommy, please come home.

The timer dinged, jolting Kim to wakefulness. Without realizing she was doing it, she brought her hands up and wiped the tears from her cheeks.

Another dialysis session was over.

IN TRUE CELEBRITY fashion, Justin made his way to No. 448. Like the other stock cars in the race, it glistened in the early-afternoon sun, the orange-and-brown Fulcrum team colors shimmering like a banked fire. The brash Turn-Rite Tools logo was emblazoned across the hood, the name spelled out on the rear quarter panels.

"See you in Victory Lane!" a fan called out.

"Good luck!" another yelled.

"You're the best!" A woman's voice surfaced above the din.

Helmet tucked under his arm, Justin waved with his free hand, a broad, confident smile plastered across his face.

"We installed the wedge," Hugo told him as the car was being rolled out of the garage by the mechanics. "You're good to go."

They'd had a dispute over installing a wedge in the right rear spring to correct the looseness—what highway drivers would call fishtailing—Justin had experienced in his practice laps earlier that morning. Hugo had insisted on increasing outside tire pressure, but the incremental increases he'd initiated hadn't resolved the problem. He'd finally given in to Justin's recommendation. Unfortunately they hadn't had enough time to test-drive the adjustment.

"I hope it works," Hugo added as Justin threw his leg over the window frame to enter the vehicle. "Let us know as soon as you do, and we'll make any further adjustments you suggest."

It was a flag of truce of sorts. As the driver, Justin had the final say on the car's configuration, but it was usual for the driver to evaluate the situation and let the crew chief and his technical people determine the solution. Hugo and Justin often discussed proposed changes, but Justin rarely if ever overrode his uncle's decision, and more often than not found himself wrong when he did. He didn't have the same level of confidence in his uncle today, however, and felt more at liberty to debate the best course of action with him. Something was definitely distracting the old man. Justin had caught him looking idly across the track to the grandstands several times. That wasn't like him.

"Will do," Justin said, trying his best to sound conciliatory.

For the life of him, Justin couldn't figure out what was going on with his uncle. Sure he was worried about Kim. Everybody was. But Hugo had always been so predictable—not in a boring way, but dependable. They'd had their disagreements from time to time. People did, and Justin figured it was especially true in a parent-child relationship. Most recently it had been over his association with Sophia Grosso, Dean Grosso's daughter, but when it came to the sport they both loved, Justin usually acceded to Hugo's judgment without it turning into a contest. After all, his uncle had been managing racing teams and evaluating races as long or longer than Justin had been alive.

He slithered through the car's open window and

adjusted the five-point safety harness that kept him snugly clutched in the customized bucket seat. Hugo handed him his fitted helmet. Justin pulled the sides of it slightly apart as he tugged it over his ears, then fastened the chin strap. In this position, with the car immobile, he felt like he was in a straitjacket, since he had very little freedom of movement. Once the race began, however, he would completely forget about physical discomfort, the sweltering heat generated by 750 horsepower and the torrents of sweat he'd be secreting over the next four hours. Only one thing would claim his concentration: the race.

He performed a radio check on his built-in headset. Clear.

He'd taken nineteenth place in his qualifying lap Friday afternoon. The overwhelming majority of winners on this track had started either in the pole position—the lead car on the inside of the double row of competitors—or were among the first ten cars.

Martinsville was the shortest track in the NASCAR Sprint Cup Series. The road surface was inconsistent, concrete in the turns and asphalt in the stunted straightaways. Maneuvering around opponents on such a short, diverse track was difficult and exhausting.

"Nineteenth isn't an ideal place to be in," Hugo had said Friday evening, "but it's not impossible. If you can finish among the top ten, you'll have accomplished something, and as far as I'm concerned, being in the top five is as good as a win. Martinsville is a tough challenge."

Justin had listened carefully as they discussed strategies for pit stops—the fewer the better—tire changes, tire pressures, maneuvering techniques and the likely biggest challengers on the track: Dean Grosso; his son, Kent; Bart and Will Branch; Jem Nordstrom; and Rafael O'Bryan.

"Forget about two-tire changes," Hugo advised. On some tracks you could get away with only changing the outside tires every other pit stop. "This track gobbles up rubber like a kid chomps an ice-cream cone. We'll go for four tires every time. Better to have to eat the extra seconds in pit stops than take a chance on a blowout and maybe a wipeout. I'll keep you posted on anyone who opts for only two. They're likely to be trouble. It's a temptation, especially toward the end of the race when everybody's trying to squeeze out every possible second."

Justin agreed, but he couldn't shake the notion that his uncle's attention wasn't completely on the race. The wedge was just one case in point. If he had installed it before the qualifying lap, Justin would probably be in a much better position. He might even have taken the pole.

CHAPTER TWELVE

SYLVIE WALKED unhurriedly along the outside perimeter of the grandstands, her senses filled with impressions, her mind occupied with memories. She hadn't been to a NASCAR track in thirty years, yet it was as if she had never been away. Oh, the trucks and vans were newer, as were the haulers, motor homes and RVs. The race track complexes were more elaborate now, too. Grandstands were bigger. Private suites capped most of them. Infield facilities were more modern, more sophisticated, better organized. The changes, however, didn't come close to matching the things that remained the same.

The air-shattering roar of finely tuned, high-powered, unmuffled engines being revved in the background. The caustic smells of lubricants, hot asphalt and scorched rubber, mingling with the savory aromas of carnival foods and charcoal fires.

She lingered to gaze at a display of souvenirs and smiled to herself. The names of teams and drivers emblazoned on the sides of model cars had certainly changed over the years, though some names, like family dynasties, persisted, Murphy and Grosso among them. The logos of their sponsors and the contours of the vehicles had undergone alteration, but the items themselves were just like the things she'd hawked at Charlotte decades ago.

If she closed her eyes, Sylvie was young again. Young and excited and scared.

She kept them open. She didn't want to go back. There was nothing to go back to.

Almost nothing.

There had been Hugo for a little while. Young. Handsome. Persistent. And so gentle. She'd never met a man who was as considerate as he had been. And funny. A clown at times.

She thought about their two recent meetings. She hadn't yet seen him smile. Had she taken that away from him? His smile. His laughter.

She studied the seating designations written on the walls of the grandstands. She didn't have to check the ticket in her purse to know her number, and she wasn't surprised to discover her seat was midway up the stand on the backstretch overlooking pit road, probably directly in front of Justin's space. Hugo must have called in some favors and paid a fortune for such a choice seat at the last minute.

People-watching had always intrigued her. Over the years she'd attended a host of country fairs where she'd sold her quilts. As a young girl she'd felt intimidated by large crowds. When she met Hugo she'd been uncomfortable in mobs of raucous race fans, but she'd ordered herself to cope. With a young daughter to support, she'd needed the work. After she left Hugo and Kim, she'd been leery of being recognized, so she'd made it a point to stay as far away from NASCAR events as possible. To her great relief she'd never seen anyone she knew.

Here, however, she felt very vulnerable, which was why she was wearing big sunglasses, a black wig, a slouch hat and unremarkable, baggy clothes.

She arrived at one of the entrance gates. People of every age and description were lining up, presenting their tickets and streaming into the fenced area. She observed several young men not far from the gate talking among themselves. From the cut of their hair and their straight bearing, it was clear they were GIs. One of them, a tall, lanky kid who couldn't be long out of his teens, was leaning on a cane.

She inched closer to listen to what they were saying.

"Sorry I wasn't able to get an infield pass for you, too, Josh," said a stocky, older man.

"That's okay, Sarge," the guy with the cane replied. "I can't believe you were able to get a ticket at all on such short notice." He held up his ticket. "This is fantastic."

"We'll meet you here after the race," a third companion reminded him.

The three started down the line to another gate and melded into the crowd. The guy with the cane—Josh?—turned and moved laboriously in the other direction.

"Excuse me," Sylvie called out to him.

He stopped and turned, a "Who? Me?" expression on his smooth face. "Yes, ma'am?"

"I saw you holding up your ticket. Is your seat in section J?"

He glanced down at the ticket in his hand and nodded to her. "Yes, ma'am. J-308."

"In the frontstretch or backstretch?" she asked anxiously.

"Um—" he glanced at his ticket "—the frontstretch, ma'am."

Sylvie closed her eyes and let out a prayerful sigh. "I wonder…would you be willing to do me a big, big favor? I know I have no right to ask this, you understand, but Mildred—she's my sister—got our tickets online, and as usual, well…I should have done it myself. You don't want to hear about the way she manages to screw up the simplest things. Anyway, she got us both tickets in section J. The only problem is her ticket is in the frontstretch and mine is in the backstretch. You would think she'd know the difference between front and back, but then you don't know Mildred. Anyway…I'm wondering if you would be willing to trade seats with me. Your seat isn't right next to Mildred's, of course, but close enough that I can probably talk someone into trading with one of us when I get there. Oh, you probably have someone waiting for you, too. This won't work." Sylvie hung her head, completely defeated.

"I've got no one waiting for me there, ma'am," the young man informed her.

"Are you sure? I mean, I wouldn't want to mess things up for you."

Five minutes later Josh was limping happily to a seat eight rows up in front of pit road, and Sylvie was on her way to climbing to row 308 on the other side of the track. She couldn't help smiling to herself as she pictured Hugo looking over into the stands and seeing a stranger sitting in the seat he had chosen for her.

She felt guilty about it, too. He wasn't a bad man. She would never have left Kim, the most precious thing in her life, with him if she'd thought he was. What he had been then, and what he was now, was an idealist. He'd been unable then to conceive of the evil his brother was capable of, and he was unable now to understand that she had no place in Kim's life. They

were both ignoring all the years of recriminations—
on both their parts—that had followed. He blamed her
for leaving; she blamed him for her *having* to.

Sylvie worked her way across the high row of
seats, found the one she'd traded for, settled into it,
extracted a pair of binoculars from her tote and
slipped the bag onto the deck behind her legs.

"Gentlemen, start your engines."

The roar of the crowd around her matched that of
the cars on the track below. She had never watched a
race from the grandstands. Before she'd met Hugo,
she'd had to stay with the truck, loaded with the souvenirs she was selling. After she and Hugo had gotten
married, she'd taken in the action from behind the wall
of pit road. Since then she'd watched it on TV and kept
up with all the teams, especially the Murphys.

For the first few laps she observed what was going
on through her sunglasses. The cars streaking by, the
excitement of the crowds, the crews behind the wall.
With a sense of anticipation and trepidation, she
stuck her sunglasses above the long, shadowy bill of
her cap and raised the binoculars to her eyes.

It took her a few seconds to focus, then a few
more to get her bearings. With growing confidence
and an unexpected sense of excitement, she zeroed
in on the pit area designated for No. 448.

The inactivity there was deceptive. Half a dozen

men in team uniform and another half a dozen in regular clothes were standing around. Barring an accident, a blowout or a mechanical problem, they wouldn't be doing anything for nearly half an hour. Then there would be a pit stop and a flurry of activity that lasted less than thirty seconds, followed once more by apparent lethargy.

She studied the faces of those she could make out through her binoculars. From TV coverage she recognized the jowly face of Dixon Rogers, the Fulcrum team owner. She moved the lenses from crew member to crew member and finally settled on the face of one man atop the war wagon.

Hugo.

Even with his features partially masked by his headset and shadowed by his long-billed cap, he looked tired. She wasn't surprised. If preoccupation with the Chase for the NASCAR Sprint Cup Series wasn't robbing him of sleep, Kim's upcoming surgery would be. And, of course, her own reappearance after so many years was undoubtedly akin to a nightmare.

He was talking to someone. She shifted her lenses to a younger man, also wearing a headset, a man with thick, dark hair and square, handsome Mediterranean features. He was looking down at someone on the other side of the monster toolbox.

He was Wade Abraham, Hugo's car chief, Kim's

fiancé. Sylvie had seen an interview he'd given several months earlier and been impressed with his confidence and articulate presentation. He came across as very intelligent, a man's man, the kind every woman admired.

Who was he speaking to on the other side of the wagon? Could it be Kim? Sylvie's heart began to pound.

But then Wade turned away from the person he was talking to, and Sylvie was unable to catch a glimpse of the person. She continued to scan the people on the far side of the divide, and finally focused on a slender young woman wearing a team T-shirt and cap who was talking to a member of the pit crew.

Rachel!

Sylvie had seen a picture of her accompanying an article in a magazine about a year ago, featuring the only woman engine builder at the NASCAR Sprint Cup Series level. The still shots hadn't done her justice, Sylvie realized. Even in the team uniform, the young woman's inescapable femininity blossomed through, as did the momentary twinkle in her green eyes when someone said something funny.

Rachel had been two years old when her mother died. Sylvie remembered Virginia lovingly showing the toddler her newborn brother, swathed in a whisper-soft flannel blanket.

"Poor Ginny," Sylvie murmured to herself, confident no one around could hear her. "If only you had persevered a little bit longer, girl. I could have solved your problem, too, on that cold, rainy night."

She was about to turn her attention away from the pretty face when she realized the young woman was talking to someone. She shifted the binoculars toward the other person…and froze.

Kim. Her Kim.

She'd seen a few pictures of her over the years in magazine articles, even caught a glimpse of her in the background of a video once, but this was the first time she'd been able to actually look into her daughter's face, an animated face, aglow with life and excitement.

Rachel made a remark and Kim laughed. Sylvie wanted to laugh with her, but the burning in her throat pulled at her mouth, made her bite her lip.

The little girl she'd abandoned, all grown up. The little girl who would no longer recognize her and would undoubtedly reject her if she did.

The years slipped away, or rather the emptiness that stretched between now and then. A little girl. A woman. The same, yet different. One innocent. The other a victim. It all seemed so unfair, yet it was real. "Oh, Kimmy baby," she murmured. A little thin, Sylvie noted, but that was probably to be expected, given her chronic health problem. It didn't detract from her beauty, only emphasized the fine precision of her bone structure. She possessed the kind of elegance that would last into advanced age.

Kim turned and the two women strolled off.

Don't go! Sylvie wanted to shout. *Let me feast my eyes on you some more.* "Don't go," she whispered. To no avail. Kim and her cousin disappeared in the maze of people and things crowding the other side of the pit wall.

Not that it would make any difference. The tears brimming in Sylvie's eyes made seeing impossible.

Kim. Her Kimmy. She'd seen her at last.

CHAPTER THIRTEEN

"PIT STOP," Hugo said into Justin's ear.

"Two more laps." He'd already made two pit stops. If he could hold out a little longer, maybe he'd only need one more. That would give him a tremendous advantage.

"You're firing on vapors now. Come in," Hugo ordered him.

Justin shot past the turnout onto pit road.

"Justin," Hugo pleaded, "you have to come in."

"One more—"

Suddenly there was a sputter, then a heart-stopping loss of power. Will Branch in the No. 467 swung around him on the right and streaked ahead like a thunderbolt.

Justin cursed, at least in his mind. Voicing it on the radio would cost him dearly.

He'd moved up eight places in more than 650 laps and was panting after tenth place—until he'd run out of gas.

He disengaged the clutch and coasted over the white line on the left, then off the paved shoulder to the narrow ribbon of dirt border. The engine had quit.

One advantage of a short track was that you were never too far from pit road and rescue. Before the car had actually dwindled to a halt, a tow truck was on its way to pick up the stalled car. The entrance to pit road was only a few dozen yards ahead.

Qualifying time not only established position in the starting lineup, but determined the pecking order in choosing locations on pit road. Like most drivers, Justin preferred to be at the head of the line. Qualifying in nineteenth place, however, hadn't given him that option. Hugo had recommended that since he couldn't be among the first five out of pit road, he should be the first one into his slot there. Justin hadn't been enthusiastic about the idea, but had decided to go along, since his chances of winning were already greatly diminished. He chose the last space on the long service line, and now he was grateful for it, since it meant his car didn't have to be pushed the entire length of the utility road.

Four fresh tires and a full gas-up. Optimum standard: fourteen seconds or less. Justin was moving again under his own power in fifteen and a half seconds. But he had lost three precious minutes getting there.

Dammit. He'd started nineteenth, worked his way up to eleventh, and now, because he hadn't trusted his uncle's judgment, he'd lost his chance, not only to finish in the top ten, but maybe even in first place. Back on the track, he was in twenty-second place and had lost a lap. He had to do something to salvage his pride. If he could at least complete the race ahead of where he'd started…

By lap 800, with 150 still to go, he had once again managed to make up his lost lap and advance six positions, thanks largely to a wreck in the lead pack that he was able to snake around unscathed. Okay, he was ahead of where he'd started, but it still wasn't good enough. He had to keep pushing. No less than tenth place was acceptable.

He was riding Brett Conroe's tail going into turn three, when Conroe suddenly lost traction and broke to the right. As Justin was inching past him, Conroe was rear-ended by Jem Nordstrom. The two outsiders went into a drift, blue-white smoke billowing from their burning tires, when Nils Booker, directly in front of Justin, went loose and began a slow rotation to the right. Unable to pass him, Justin had no alternative but to apply his brakes.

No sooner had they entered the straightaway beyond turn four than Haze Clifford tapped Justin's inside back bumper, spinning him out down the short

frontstretch. Fighting to regain control, Justin slithered along the outside wall, miraculously attained
forward reorientation and floored the gas pedal.

Too late. Finnegan Jarvis and Mitch Volmer glided
by on the inside, closely followed by a stream of
other cars. Justin found himself on the outside
looking in as car after car passed him on the left.

He entered Turn One wide, remained there
through turn two, was passed by three more cars and
finally nosed his way to the inside just as he was
entering turn three.

For the last fifty laps he battled his way through
the second pack, gaining a position, losing two,
gaining two, losing one.

"Where am I?" he asked disconsolately as the
white flag fluttered ahead, announcing the last lap.

"Twenty-ninth," his uncle answered.

THE MOOD WAS SOMBER as the team plane took off.
They would be back in Charlotte in less than an hour
and could be home within two.

Hugo sat beside Kim in his usual place, a plush
leather-upholstered lounger in the forward section of
the cabin, and sipped a scotch on the rocks. He
wasn't much of a drinker, never had been, and
couldn't remember the last time he'd had more than
one beer in a row. Even this shot of hard liquor was

so watered down that he'd probably have to chug it on an empty stomach to get much of a buzz.

The day had been an unmitigated disaster. Sylvie hadn't turned up as he'd hoped, though even if she had, he knew there was no chance she would have agreed to meet Kim. But he'd wanted to give her an opportunity to at least see her daughter, in person, if only from a distance. Maybe then, he'd prayed, she'd relent later when he proposed again that they meet. He'd scanned the grandstands in the section where he'd managed to obtain seats, thanks to Dixon Rogers, and found, instead, a young man in her place.

"Uncle Hugo?"

He looked up at Rachel standing over him, hand in hand with her husband. Peyton Reese looked sheepish and slightly embarrassed, a sharp contrast to his usual brash self.

"We have something we want to tell you and the rest of the family," she said. She spoke loudly enough for Justin and Sophia, who were sitting in equally luxurious recliners on the other side of the aisle, to hear.

In a moment of instant insight, Hugo knew what they were about to tell him, but decided to let his niece say it. "And that is?"

Rachel gazed into her husband's eyes and said, "I'm pregnant. We're going to have a baby!"

Hugo grinned and rose to his feet. Kim, sitting

beside him, jumped to hers and threw her arms around her cousin, while Justin shot out of his seat, grabbed his brother-in-law's hand and yanked it vigorously.

"That's fantastic," Kim said. "I'm so happy for you." There was a tear in her voice.

"I'm going to be an uncle!" Justin spouted.

Hugo saw Wade, who'd been sitting a few rows back discussing the day's race with a couple of team members, dash to Kim's side. The longing in her eyes, as she tried to smile at him, nearly broke Hugo's heart.

One of the first things his daughter had asked when she was diagnosed with kidney failure was whether dialysis would prevent her from having children. She hadn't met Wade yet and had never discussed marriage with her father, but he knew she wanted a family if she found the right man. He'd overheard her tell a friend some years earlier that she wanted a house full of children, that she was going to prove she could be a better mother to them than her own mother had been to her.

The medical verdict then and now was that trying to have kids was highly ill-advised as long as she was on dialysis, but that after a kidney transplant, it would be possible for her to have children. Her prenatal condition, however, would have to be very carefully monitored.

As Wade folded his arms around her, Hugo saw

the shimmer in her eyes, even as she smiled. She was genuinely happy for her cousin and wished her all the best, but the longing he also saw on her face made it clear that the sooner she got her kidney transplant the better.

"I'm going to be a great-uncle," Hugo added, suddenly feeling very old. He enfolded his niece in a hug, kissed her on the cheek, then waited his turn to congratulate Peyton.

"That's wonderful news," he said, and meant it. Life went on, as it always had. He prayed that the lives of these young people and the baby they were bringing into the world would be blessed with the kind of happiness he'd once had, for a very brief time, and that theirs would never end.

Sophia, still an outsider to this family, if no longer quite the enemy, stood up, waited for an appropriate opening and gave Rachel a big hug.

"I'm really happy for you," she said.

Rachel smiled and thanked her.

Sophia retrieved her glass of red wine and held it up. "I propose a toast. To new life and the joys of family."

Justin and Wade topped off their drinks from Hugo's bottle of twelve-year-old single-malt scotch, while Kim and Rachel contented themselves with sparkling mineral water, in a toast to the latest member of the family.

Hugo chuckled. "I guess I understand now why you've been a bit—"

"Don't you dare say it," Rachel warned him, her eyes twinkling but narrowed.

"What?" He was grinning.

"Hormonal!"

He laughed. "I was going to say high-spirited."

"Sure you were, Dad. Sure you were." Kim chortled, as a tear ran down her cheek.

CHAPTER FOURTEEN

MONDAY WAS the team's normal down day, the one day of the week when they got a break. But Kim was going into the hospital on Tuesday, so Hugo called a special meeting for Monday afternoon to discuss Sunday's race and the upcoming schedule.

"Yesterday was a disaster," Justin said. He was sitting in the middle of the long conference table in the meeting room next to Hugo's office.

"Yes, it was," Hugo agreed from the head of the table, "and it shouldn't have been. You drove a good race, moved up steadily and had a chance to continue to move up, until you refused to come in for a pit stop."

"I would have started a lot better than in nineteenth place if the wedge I'd asked for had been installed!" Justin snapped back. "Based on the way Rachel had that engine purring, I might even have been able to take the pole."

"I accept full responsibility for that," Hugo said.

"I should have respected your instincts. It was your butt in the seat. You drove a near-perfect race in the first half, Justin. You were in a position to take the lead when—"

Rachel threw up her hands. Normally an engine builder wouldn't be part of this type of meeting, but she was also family.

"Everybody stop and take a deep breath," she ordered loudly enough to command attention. "There's enough blame to go around, but if you two are going to play childish games about who was more at fault, the rest of us might just as well go home and enjoy the rest of the day, because we're not going to accomplish a darn thing here."

The two men stopped, turned and stared at her with their mouths hanging open.

Hugo broke into a chuckle. "She's right. Impending motherhood seems to have given her rare wisdom."

"Don't you dare patronize me!" she said.

"Sorry," he said with more humor than sincerity, then grew serious again. "For the record," he said to Justin, "I acknowledge you were right about the wedge. Can we get past it?"

"I'm sorry, too," Justin said. "The truth is I'm more ticked at myself than you. Tomorrow is Kim's big day. I guess it has us all on edge."

"YOU LOOK LIKE HELL," Sylvie said when she opened the door to her ex-husband.

"Thank you. May I come in?"

She shook her head and stepped aside. "What's wrong? Is Kim—"

"Kim is fine." He stood in the middle of the shabby room and waited for her to close the door. "I didn't sleep very well last night. Tomorrow—" He stopped. "How are you feeling?"

"I'm all right," she assured him. "But you obviously aren't. Can I get you something? I was going to say to *eat,* but maybe I ought to say to *drink* instead. I have some whiskey around here somewhere."

"I don't want anything."

"What's the matter, Hugo?"

"You didn't come to the race yesterday."

A diversion, she decided. Something else was bothering him. She walked around him and went to the refrigerator. "Actually I did. I just didn't sit where you wanted me to."

He snorted and rolled his eyes. "Still don't trust me, huh?" He paused a moment. "So you saw her."

"Thank you for arranging it," she said as she poured two glasses of iced tea. He'd drink his when she gave it to him. "I figured that was your real reason for giving me the ticket."

"Maybe I just wanted you to enjoy a NASCAR race, Sylvie."

"Maybe. And I did. Very much." She handed him a glass. Their fingers touched briefly. She wanted to erase the memory of how those fingers had felt on her body so long ago. No, that wasn't true. She didn't *want* to forget, she *needed* to. No one had ever touched her like that before…or since. But she couldn't will amnesia. At least, she hadn't been able to so far, though she'd tried. "She's lovely, Hugo. You can be proud of the way you brought her up."

He didn't seem to know how to react to the compliment. At last he said simply, "Thank you."

She waved him to the easy chair he'd occupied the first time he'd come here, while she took her accustomed place at the quilting frame.

"Is it worry about tomorrow that has you so glum? She's going to be all right, Hugo. I can feel it in my bones." In fact, she hadn't slept much last night, either, worrying about her little girl.

He took a swallow from his glass. "Come with me and meet her."

She wasn't surprised by the suggestion. "We've already been through this, Hugo. You know it's not going to happen."

"She deserves to know you care. After all these years, she needs to know."

Sylvie shook her head. "No good would come of it. You know what I have to do and why I have to do it. You also made a promise to let me go."

She deposited her sweaty glass on the side table and folded her hands in her lap. "I was wrong to not trust you with the truth years ago. Please don't make me regret trusting you with it now."

He gazed steadily into her eyes, and the hunger she saw in his cried out so acutely she was afraid she would start weeping again. She'd been teary-eyed all day long, thinking about her daughter, thinking about Hugo, remembering the good times, regretting all the time lost. Maybe if she'd come back years ago, when Kim was old enough to understand, and set the record straight… But then she would still be in prison for Troy's death. What good would that have done anybody? This way, Kim didn't have to live with the shame of having a mother who was incarcerated for killing a man.

Hugo set his glass aside and rose from the well-worn chair. "Do you need a ride to the hospital tomorrow morning?" he asked.

"I'm fine, Hugo," she insisted. "Really."

"I'll stop in to see you before the operation."

"Please don't—"

"I'll be discreet. I promise."

What frightened her was that she *wanted* him to

come by. She wasn't worried about the surgery she would undergo. The chances of complications weren't on her side of the transplant procedure. But she'd never been in a hospital before. Kim had been born at home with her mother and a neighbor woman as midwives. Seeing a friendly face, Hugo's, would do a lot to reassure her.

He stood up, carried his glass, half-empty, to the counter on his way to the door, then turned around and walked over to her. He bent and kissed her gently on the cheek.

"I'll see you in the morning," he said and let himself out.

SHE CRIED after he left, cried as hard as she had in years. She cried for what had been lost and could never be again. She cried for Kim, the little girl she had left behind. She cried for Hugo, who had accepted a burden he hadn't bargained for but had accepted unconditionally, wholeheartedly.

She cried for herself.

For three decades she had tried to deny the feelings she had for him. Even when she saw him standing in her doorway, and her heart leaped at the sight of him, she had tried to deny that she still loved him. She'd conjured up all sorts of reasons for not feeling what she felt, but the truth was, she did love him. She always had; she always would.

Hugo Murphy was the only truly good man she had ever known. Her father had been cruel and vindictive. His best friend's son had been worse. Troy Murphy had been willing to use physical intimidation to get what he wanted. But Hugo had been a gentle man—and he still was. In spite of his failures, she felt safe with him. He would have protected her back then, if she had told him of the threat. But she had been too young to understand. All he'd needed was to have his eyes opened. Not helping him see was her failure.

How many times had she told herself that she'd gotten over him? How many times had she lied? Now she had seen him, experienced the sweet delight of his presence, felt him touch her. She couldn't lie anymore. She loved him. She wanted him in her life. Yet she couldn't stay.

CHAPTER FIFTEEN

HUGO COULDN'T remember when he had last set his alarm clock. An early riser by nature, he was in the habit of telling himself when he had to get up and waking within a few minutes of the designated time. Even so, rising at five-thirty in the morning was rare, but he didn't want to arrive late at the hospital for Kim's seven-thirty admission. He might just as well have skipped setting the alarm, though, because he was up and dressed and drinking his second cup of coffee when five-thirty rolled around.

Dr. Peterson had been emphatic that the prognosis for a successful transplant operation was excellent, the match between the donor and Kim being nearly perfect. No one needed to worry, he said, because Kim was in good hands—his. Hugo didn't consider himself a cynical person, but his reaction had been that if it was such a slam dunk, why was it necessary to offer so many reassurances?

Kim and Wade were already at the registration

office when Hugo arrived at the hospital, waiting for the clerk to call her name. Hugo was at the refreshment bar in the corner pouring himself another cup of coffee when Justin, slightly out of breath, showed up with Sophia. Barely a minute later Rachel and Peyton arrived.

The clerk called Kim's name.

Hugo fidgeted as the clerk verified the patient's name and address, explained the significance of several pieces of paper she handed over for her to sign, then placed an identification bracelet on her right wrist. A volunteer personally escorted the gaggle to a staff elevator, which took them up to the fourth floor. There, they were turned over to a nurse, who led them to a stark patient's room. Everyone was asked to wait outside while Kim changed out of her street clothes into a white-and-pink cotton hospital gown that opened in the back.

Sylvie would be going through the same process more discreetly, Hugo imagined, except she would be doing it alone. He should be with her, if not to hold her hand—something he would gladly do—but to at least assure her she wasn't alone.

Kim was sitting up in the bed, a sheet pulled to her waist, when the entourage was invited into the room.

"Cool threads," Justin teased with a grin.

Rachel walked up to her cousin and fingered the

snap sleeves. "What do you think?" she asked, leaning closer to examine the faded fabric. "Flowers or bunny rabbits? I can't tell."

Wade smiled at Kim nervously. Peyton stood by mutely.

Hugo caught himself recalling when the woman in the bed had been a girl of five about to have her tonsils out only a few months after Sylvie had disappeared....

"Where's Mommy?" she'd asked. "Why isn't she here? You said she was coming back."

He'd run out of excuses, explanations and evasions.

"Your mommy loves you very much, but she can't be here just now." He'd stopped promising she would show up soon.

"Will she be here when I wake up?"

How many times had the child asked that question before going to sleep at night? At first he'd said she would. Then he'd said he hoped she would. Then he'd said he didn't know. Eventually the sad little girl had stopped asking, but Hugo knew the question was never far from her lips. He'd been tempted to hate Sylvie at those times, but he could never bring himself to do it. Maybe she was dead, as everyone seemed to think. Maybe she'd been kidnapped or had amnesia. There had to be a logical explanation for her vanishing the way she had. Sylvie, his Sylvie, wouldn't just walk away from Kim and him without a reason!

Kim had just turned seven when Hugo filed the papers to legally adopt her. There was no one to contest the motion and it went through quietly. He wasn't a public figure yet, so the media had paid no attention when the request and judgment were published in small print among the legal notices in the local paper. To Kim the change in status had been transparent. She'd been calling him Daddy since the day he and Sylvie had gotten married.

Kim was about ten when she came home from school one day and announced that she hated her mother. Hugo was at a loss as to how to respond. He understood her anger at her mother's abandonment, even shared it. He had to keep reminding himself that he didn't know what had happened to Sylvie, and it was unfair of him to condemn her until he found out. He did his best to convince his daughter that she had every right to hate her mother's disappearance but not to hate her mother. The distinction was subtle for a ten-year-old, but Kim seemed to grasp it.

After that, however, whenever she was asked about her mother, Kim always replied that she was dead. At first Hugo tried to discourage her, saying they didn't know that was true, but Kim argued that as far as she was concerned, her mother was dead, and if she didn't tell strangers that, what should she tell them? Hugo didn't have a good answer.

It wasn't until Kim had turned sixteen that she started asking for the details of her mother's disappearance. Hugo was as honest as possible; he told her about Rachel and Justin's mother's suicide, about their father being killed in an accident and that a month later Sylvie disappeared.

"Did you try to find her?" Kim asked.

"Of course I did. I had detectives looking for her for several years."

"Do you think she's dead?"

That was a tough one. Part of him said she must be, almost wished she was because it would explain her disappearance and make it forgivable. Another part of him simply refused to believe it.

"I don't know," he'd replied, the answer honest but unsatisfying.

He'd waited for Kim to say something more, make a statement, ask another question, but she'd only nodded and walked away. They rarely mentioned Sylvie after that. Hugo understood her ambivalence. There had occasionally been sightings of Sylvie that Hugo followed up on, the most recent one being in Alaska. Kim showed interest in the results, but no great emotion when they turned out to be cases of mistaken identity or dead ends.

Oddly, she hadn't speculated about who her kidney donor might be, why a total stranger would offer to give her a piece of her body. Nor had she proposed meeting the woman to thank her or even writing a card to be forwarded to the anonymous person saving her life.

Did that mean Kim suspected the donor might be her mother? It seemed the only explanation for such ingratitude from a person who had always been gracious and polite.

How, then, would she react if she found out the donor really was her mother?

SHE HAD BEEN waiting for him, afraid for once that he wouldn't keep his word and show up, that she would be left all alone in this foreign place. She shouldn't want…no, crave his company, feel satisfied when he was with her. She treasured their moments together. Somehow the rest of the world, its cares and sorrows, receded when he was with her, as if the two of them alone, together, could control their destiny.

Barely seconds after he entered the room, a matronly nurse charged in behind him, demanding he leave immediately and threatening to call security if he didn't.

"There is a no-visitors sign posted on the door for a reason," she informed him.

Sylvie saw the consternation mixed with amusement play on Hugo's face. Clearly the nurse didn't recognize the Fulcrum Motors crew chief. Not that it would likely have made any difference. Rules were rules, this woman's demeanor announced plainly. Sylvie also understood that if Hugo put up any resistance and was recognized, Sylvie's anonymity as the organ donor for his daughter would probably be blown.

"That's all right," Sylvie told the nurse. "He's the one exception."

The nurse huffed, gave the interloper a dirty look and made her exit.

"You shouldn't be here," Sylvie told him.

"Our secret is safe," he assured her from the foot of the bed. He looked ill at ease, which was unusual for a man who normally exuded control. This was an important day for him. His daughter's life and well-being were at stake. "The staff already knows you are the anonymous donor. My being here, assuming they know who I am, doesn't change anything."

"How is she?" Sylvie asked, keeping her hands folded in her lap. She was particularly aware that she was wearing only the yellow-and-pink hospital gown, that beneath it she was naked, that he was standing only a few feet away.

"Holding up like a trouper," he said proudly. "Her fiancé and cousins are with her." He gazed into Sylvie's eyes. "How are *you?*"

They'd reached the point where meaningless

words accomplished nothing. Time was not on their side. She answered honestly.

"I'm not sure," she said. "Physically I'm perfectly all right. Good country stock, this." She made a rolling motion with her hands as if displaying her body. "Emotionally—" she shrugged "—I'm not nearly as certain. Don't misunderstand. I'm not having second thoughts. I'm happy about what I'm doing. I also know it's not particularly dangerous— for me." She nestled her shoulders into the pillows behind her. "I'm thinking, though, how much better it might be for everyone…if I didn't wake up."

"Don't say that!" Obviously shaken, he moved to the side of the bed. He reached for her hands and took them in both of his. She tried to pull away but not hard enough to convince him she meant it. "I hope you don't really believe that."

"That's my dilemma," she replied with a wan sigh. "I don't know if I do or not." She gazed at him. He gave her a smile that was strangely peaceful, yet filled with sadness. He was feeling what she was feeling, she realized, a will to fight, yet a sense of resignation. The next hours were out of their hands. They could cope. They must. But ultimately they had to accept.

"The healthy part of me wants to live," she continued, "and I'm reasonably sure I will. But another part of me, the moral part perhaps, keeps asking why I should go on."

Fear widened his eyes, but she saw grudging respect, too.

"There's always hope," he said softly, firmly.

"Of what, Hugo? Think about it. This is all I can do, the best I can do. I can give Kim something unique, something that will make a real difference in her life. I don't regret the decision, not for a minute, and I won't after the operation. In fact, I think I've lived all these years for this very moment, for this opportunity to say I care."

She extracted her hands from his grip and smoothed out the sheet folded across her waist.

"But then what, Hugo? I'll have done all I can. I'll have served my purpose. What's kept me going all these years is the hope that I could fulfill some destiny. Now it's here, and I'm happy to do it. But once done, there's no further point for my existence."

"That's not true! You matter, Sylvie. You matter to me."

Her heart filled to overflowing with gratitude. "Thank you, Hugo." She'd promised herself she wouldn't let this meeting, maybe their last, bring tears, but they were dangerously close. "After all I've done to you…your saying that says more about you than it does about me." She yanked a tissue out of a nearby dispenser. She wouldn't let herself cry, but just in case…

She perked up. "But you don't have to worry about me going anywhere." She poked herself with her thumb. "Good stock, remember? I'll still be here at the end of the day."

"Come with me to meet her, Sylvie," he quietly pleaded. "Give her a chance to get to know you. I know she'll love you."

Love. How long she'd waited to hear that word again. The emotions that flooded her thrilled and appalled her. She wished she wasn't in the bed, trapped, so she could turn away from him.

She fixed her eyes on him again. "The answer is still no. I won't meet her. Let her live her life with my blessing."

There was a tap on the door. A nurse entered the room. "We're ready to take you now."

CHAPTER SIXTEEN

THEY SAT in the surgical waiting room. Hugo, Wade, Rachel, Peyton. Sophia Grosso had come with Justin and asked Hugo's permission to stay. He let her, of course. Old animosities seemed petty in the face of a contemporary life crisis.

For the first hour everybody talked. Mostly about NASCAR, but with an undeclared agreement not to discuss last Sunday's race. The same applied to the upcoming race in Atlanta and the Grosso/Murphy feud, which limited subject matter to technical details, racing history and gossip. The challenge of NASCAR trivia still kept the conversation lively.

The second hour was spent in silence, except for the frequent phone calls from Kim's best friend, Isabel, who was stuck out of town on business. The men devoted themselves to the selection of sports magazines scattered around the room. Rachel and Sophia had had the foresight to bring books—

reading was something they had in common, though their tastes were different—so they tucked themselves into opposite corners of the matching couches and plunged into their books.

Patience and nonchalance finally gave out in the third hour. Everyone started taking turns pacing, visiting the water fountain, examining the fine print on the art reproductions and medical posters dotting the walls.

"We should hear something pretty soon now, right?" Justin asked no one in particular.

"Dr. Peterson said removing the donor organ would take about an hour," Wade replied. "Then there'd be about two hours to implant it in the recipient."

"That's the way I remember it, too," Hugo said. "The whole process should take about three hours."

Wade looked at the clock on the wall. "It's only been two and a half—"

"If they started on time," Rachel interjected.

"Better they take longer than expected and do it right," her brother said.

No one disagreed.

"What about the donor?" Sophia asked a few minutes later.

Everyone stopped and looked at her. She took them all in at a glance, clearly uncertain why the question should provoke such a shocked reaction.

"What about her?" Hugo asked, coming to a standstill by the water fountain.

"We're the only ones here. Doesn't she have anyone waiting for her?"

"Maybe there's another waiting room for donors," Justin suggested.

"Probably is," Wade said. "Since she wanted to be anonymous. That'd be hard to do if we were all in the same waiting room."

"Of course," Sophia concluded, "you're right. I hadn't thought of that." She paused. Then, "I wonder who she is."

"Whoever she is," Wade declared, "I sure am grateful to her."

Hugo was relieved when he realized no one seemed interested in pursuing that line of speculation further. It surprised him that very little had been said about the identity or motives of the mysterious donor. It was a relief, Hugo told himself, but it was also sad and disappointing that everyone was so focused on the recipient that they were ignoring the generous giver.

He looked up and was amazed to see Dr. Peterson standing in the doorway, wearing green scrubs, a matching cloth cap on his head, a white mask dangling from his neck.

"Let's sit down," he said, and waved everyone to the corner where the two couches were. He pulled a wooden armchair away from the wall and turned it so he could face them.

"Everything went without a hitch," he said with a proud grin. "Kim is doing fine. She tolerated the procedure very well. The donor organ was as pink and pretty as you could ask for. The connection of the renal arteries was performed with no problem. When we released the clamps the new organ infused instantly. Everything is working perfectly. The next twenty-four hours will be critical, but I don't anticipate any problems."

Everyone started speaking at once, like a team that had just won a race.

"And the donor?" Hugo asked through the enthusiastic hubbub. "How is she?"

"She'll make a full recovery," Peterson informed him.

A wave of relief rolled over Hugo. Mother and daughter were all right.

"When can we see Kim?" Rachel asked before her uncle could work the same question past the lump in his throat.

"She's in recovery now and will be there for another hour or so, then we'll move her into the surgical ICU. You'll be able to see her there one at a time, but only for a minute or two. She'll be groggy and disoriented, so don't worry if she doesn't respond to you the way you expect. Tomorrow she'll be more lucid."

"How long will you keep her in ICU?" Justin asked.

"A day or two. We need to monitor her very closely for the first twenty-four hours at least. Then we'll be able to move her to a private room."

"When can she go home?" Wade asked.

"Plan on her staying here at least ten days, maybe two weeks. We'll want to keep running tests to make sure everything is functioning as it should."

How IRONIC it would be, Hugo thought, if Kim and Sylvie happened to be placed in neighboring beds in the ICU. Mother and daughter. Donor and recipient. Lying right next to each other. Worlds apart.

It wasn't until later, however, that he learned that because Sylvie didn't require the same degree of close scrutiny as Kim, she was never sent to the ICU, but had been moved directly from recovery to a private room.

The others had already left the hospital for the night when Hugo stopped off to see Sylvie. She was sleeping, the dim night-light casting her features in shadowed relief. He remembered the pleasure he used to experience lying beside her, watching her sleep, the feeling of how lucky he was to find her. He hadn't given a thought to the possibility of losing her, and because he'd taken her for granted, he had lost her. He didn't want to do that again.

He walked to the side of her bed and held her hand with both of his. It felt cool. He hoped that meant his touch felt warm to her.

Her eyelids fluttered. She gazed at him and smiled, then slipped back into peaceful slumber.

"Thank you," he murmured. "Our daughter is fine. I love you."

The words were out before he even realized he'd said them, but once spoken, he knew they were true. In spite of everything, he still loved this woman. He stroked her hand, waited, wished for some response. But there was none. She was dead to the world—a metaphor he instantly rejected. She was alive, and she made him feel alive. Thanks to her, their daughter was alive, as well. But it wasn't Kim he was thinking of at that moment. It was Sylvie, just Sylvie. He'd been running on empty too long. He needed her back, filling his world.

He ran his thumb over her hand. "I want another chance, Sylvie." He could hear the tremor in his voice and wondered if she could, too. "I want a chance to prove that I really love you."

It was almost ten in the evening when he finally arrived at home. He hadn't eaten, but he wasn't hungry. He was tired, but he was restless, too, like a man who'd just driven a 500-mile NASCAR race. He needed sleep but doubted he would get any.

He had told Sylvie he loved her. She'd been asleep when he said it. She probably hadn't heard him and would no doubt reject the declaration if she had, but he had said it, and he'd meant it.

How could he ever find his way through the warren of miscalculations and twisted emotions their lives had become? This woman, who had killed his brother and abandoned her daughter, who'd been the torment of his life for more than half of it… If Kim hadn't gotten sick he would never have known Sylvie was still alive. She loved her daughter enough to undergo life-threatening surgery, but she certainly didn't love him.

I love you.

He couldn't remember the last time he had said those words to her. But he'd said them now.

I love you.

He went upstairs to his bedroom, ran the shower and stepped into it, then he adjusted the multiple streams of warm water and stood among them, lost in thought. In a matter of days, two weeks at most, Sylvie would be gone from his life again. This time, he vowed, he wouldn't let her slip away.

He donned pajamas and a dressing gown, went down to the kitchen and poured himself a glass of milk.

Searching in the pantry, he found an unopened package of cookies. He always kept some on hand for Kim.

He dipped one in the milk and remembered that he'd learned about cookies and milk from Sylvie. He, Sylvie and Kim would share them at the counter of their kitchenette in the trailer. It had been their time to laugh and giggle. Did Kim still think about her mother when she had cookies and milk?

Upstairs again, he crawled into his big, solitary bed, convinced he wouldn't be able to sleep. The next thing he knew, the room was filled with light. The sun was up.

He wasn't sure when he'd reached his decision. He knew only that it was the right one. He made a phone call, dressed, climbed into his SUV and went to the downtown offices of Sloan Wycombe, Esquire.

CHAPTER SEVENTEEN

LATE WEDNESDAY afternoon, twenty-six hours after her surgery, Kim was transferred from the surgical intensive-care unit to a private room on the sixth floor, a room already overflowing with plants, bouquets, balloons, stuffed animals and get-well cards from family, friends and team members. One of the biggest bouquets was from Isabel Rogers, Kim's best friend, who was disappointed that she couldn't be at Kim's side. Even bigger, however, was the display from her father, Dixon Rogers, the owner of Fulcrum Motors. Hugo chuckled at the sight of it. The old skinflint had outdone himself, and he appreciated it.

Kim had already been up and walking several times by then. She admitted to feeling a bit shaky and weak, but the exhilaration of knowing the operation had been performed without complication and that her prognosis was excellent had her spirits soaring. Dr. Peterson had warned, however, that initial progress didn't always equate to long-term, permanent success. They would be monitoring her very closely for a long time. Rejection could occur without warning and for no apparent reason, maybe even years from now.

Wade spent as much of his spare time with her as he could squeeze away from his car-chief responsibilities, even taking hospital meals with her.

"The grub isn't all that bad," he told Hugo early Wednesday evening as the food trays were being removed. "Chicken and dumplings this evening with corn bread."

Hugo chuckled. "Sounds like good, down-home cooking to me." Nothing compared to Sylvie's, of course.

"Your mother's is better," Kim told Wade.

Hugo stayed just long enough to assure himself that his daughter was doing well, was comfortable and didn't need anything. Then he kissed her goodnight and strolled to the elevator. Pleased to find he had the car completely to himself, he pressed the button for the fifth floor. On five he got off and sauntered casually to Sylvie's room. The nurse on duty nodded a greeting.

Sylvie was sitting up in bed, reading a magazine. The volume was muted on the wall-mounted TV. A classic black-and-white movie was playing.

She looked up at his entrance and smiled. "Thank

you for the flowers, Hugo," she said sincerely. "You remembered my favorite color. They're lovely."

He'd had a large bouquet of pale violet roses delivered to her room. The card had wished her a speedy recovery but contained no signature. The overflowing vase dominated the small alcove between the room's two windows.

He was tempted to say he hadn't sent them, then tease her about having a secret admirer.

"How are you feeling?" he asked.

"They tell me I'm doing fine." His frown told her she hadn't answered his question. "I'm tired," she admitted, "but otherwise I have no complaints. They've already had me up and walking around."

"Are you in pain?"

Her shrug answered his question more than her words. "Tender where they made the incision, but I guess that's to be expected. Nothing I can't handle."

"Have they given you anything for it?"

She held up a black cable with a press button on the end. "Meds on demand."

He suspected she rarely used it. On the few occasions he'd been hospitalized for broken or bruised body parts, he'd done his best not to indulge in the powerful narcotics they made available, partly because he worried about getting addicted and partly because toughing it out was supposed to prove something. He wasn't sure what. Stupidity maybe. He'd never found any virtue in pain, but there seemed to be some kind of mysterious pride in enduring it. He wondered at the logic.

"I stopped by earlier today and late last evening, but you were sleeping both times."

She closed the home-decorating magazine she'd been perusing and left it on her lap. "I'm sorry I missed you. But you really don't have to visit, Hugo. It would be better if you didn't. If the wrong people recognize you, it could raise questions that are best left unasked. Think of how embarrassed Kim would be if word got back to her that you'd been visiting the woman who's given her a kidney, when she herself hadn't. She wouldn't be very happy with you."

Sylvie was right. He also recognized when he was being manipulated and chose to smile rather than be offended by her rejection of his company. Maybe it was his own arrogant pride. Maybe it was wishful thinking, but he sensed she secretly welcomed his visit. The nature of their relationship had changed from when she first opened her apartment door and found him standing there. Mutual fear and distrust had given way to emotions that seemed more akin to sympathy and respect. That wasn't love, of course, but it was a first step.

Had she heard what he'd told her last night? He

felt certain she wouldn't acknowledge it even if she had, but he couldn't help wondering…and hoping.

"How is she?" No need to specify who *she* referred to.

"Doing great," he told her. "Dr. Peterson is very pleased. All the tests keep coming back positive. There's no indication of organ rejection, and in spite of all the medication being pumped into her, she looks and says she feels better than she did before the surgery. A lot of it is probably wishful thinking, because she is a little doped up, but the change in her attitude alone is remarkable."

"How do you mean?"

Hugo thought for a moment. "She's always been a positive, upbeat person, someone who looks forward to what life holds. But these past months, since she was diagnosed with acute kidney failure… I don't know how to describe it exactly, but she'd developed a fatalism in her manner, a resignation that the future might be short. She's more relaxed now, more confident about the future. Of course, Wade may have something to do with it, too."

Sylvie's eyes misted. "I'm glad."

She'd given her daughter hope. What better gift could there be?

Hugo wanted to suggest again that Sylvie go with him and meet Kim, but he could see from the warning look in her eyes that she was expecting him to ask and was ready to reject the idea. He didn't want to break this warm spell. He still had time.

"Is there anything I can get for you?" he asked.

"Nothing." She paused, shoved the magazine aside and clasped her hands together in her lap. "Hugo, please don't come to see me anymore. You're just making it more difficult for both of us. I know how you feel."

"You do?"

"I also know how Kim feels. Nothing is going to change. My mind is made up. I'm going to do what has to be done." She gazed at him gently, fondly. "Thank you for the flowers and for the good wishes. I'll never forget them." Her expression suddenly changed. "Now please leave."

The abruptness and intensity of her request stunned him. He started to protest, to tell her that he loved her and that nothing was going to change that, either. But he wasn't angling for a confrontation, not about his love for her. Whether she could ever love him was another matter. She felt something for him, that much he knew, but love went deeper than feelings, deeper than desire. Real love had to be earned....

They'd been getting along so well, actually beginning to establish a comfort zone. She said she knew how he felt. Did that mean she'd heard what he'd said the night before? Had saying those words repelled her, scared her?

He studied her, the remarkably smooth skin that showed more color today than it had last night, the tiny hints of age creeping into the corners of her eyes. How strange, he thought. As unapproachable and distant as she insisted on being, the corners of her mouth didn't turn down with bitterness, though she had every right to be bitter, every right to rage against the life fate had dealt her.

Another moment passed.

"Get some rest," he said softly as he leaned forward and pressed a kiss to her forehead. "You've earned it."

She remained still, passive. He turned and left the room. He hadn't said he wouldn't be back.

"I WISH YOU WEREN'T leaving tomorrow," Kim complained Wednesday evening, as she clasped Wade's big, strong hand. "Or rather, I wish I could go to Atlanta with you, instead of having to be stuck in bed."

He chuckled as he leaned forward and kissed her. "You must be getting better. You've been stuck in bed less than two days. Give yourself a break." He looked into her eyes. "I wish you were coming with me, too, but I want you getting better even more. There'll be other races. Plenty of them, and we're going to share them together."

She brought his hand up and kissed it. "I know," she murmured. The truth was she didn't have the energy to do much of anything at this point. A short walk down the hall brought her back to her bed for an hour-long nap.

"You'll be able to watch the race on the TV with your dad."

She was proud that Wade would be filling in as Justin's crew chief in Atlanta. He'd filled in for Hugo at Dover and Kansas and done so well he was now slated to get his own Fulcrum Motors team in the NASCAR Nationwide Series next season. Screw up this crucial race in Atlanta, though, and Dixon Rogers might decide to pull the plug. Rogers wasn't a vindictive man, just an astute businessman who demanded peak performance.

"I appreciate your dad's confidence in me," Wade acknowledged. "I'll do my best not to let him down, but he's the one who should be going with us to Atlanta. This is his team, after all. He built it. He's the real crew chief."

Hugo's request that Wade take over as crew chief in Atlanta had come as a surprise to everyone. Granted, Kim had just had major surgery and he'd always been very protective of her, but it wasn't as though he had to personally monitor her activities or guard her impulses the way he did last weekend at

Martinsville. She was in a hospital with people monitoring everything she did.

Only one conclusion came to Kim's mind that might explain her father's uncharacteristic behavior, something they had never actually talked about—that her mother had returned. That somewhere close by, her mother was also lying in a bed, recovering from surgery. That it was her mother's kidney now nestled inside her.

Kim rarely spoke about the woman who had given her birth, then abandoned her, but Sylvie Ketchum had never been completely eradicated from her mind. Always there were doubts. Did her mother just not love her? Had she, Kim, done something to make her mother reject her? Was someone else responsible for her disappearance? Was she even alive? It was the uncertainty that had been the worst torture.

At home Kim had a few faded snapshots of her mother that her father had given her years ago, pictures of a beautiful young woman. Kim didn't look at those photos much anymore. She didn't need to. The images were burned deep into her memory, although the night before she was admitted to the hospital, while Wade was sleeping, she had secretly taken them out and studied them.

She barely remembered her mother. *Mommy* was more an impression than a real person, a feeling of warmth and protection, of being treasured and loved. For years Kim had asked herself what she had done to drive her mother away. When she was old enough for reason to kick in and to be told that a four-year-old child couldn't have done anything to deserve being abandoned, the desolation had turned to rage. Had it not been for Hugo, she might well have gone down a different road. Instead of devoting herself to study and becoming an almost reclusive scholar, she could have exploded into self-destructive behavior. The temptations had been there. Hugo had guided her away from them.

He'd always been there for her. He'd never stinted in his love and support. More than once Kim had wondered how her mother could have left him. Certainly not for someone better. It had taken Kim a long time to find Wade, because she knew exactly what kind of man she wanted.

Now Hugo was acting strangely, and Kim had to wonder if it was because Sylvie had come back.

It was the only logical explanation for why Hugo was staying here when he should be in Atlanta helping Justin win the NASCAR Sprint Cup Series championship.

How long had she been back? How long had Hugo known where she was? So many questions filled Kim's head that it began to ache. Better not to think about it, she told herself. Sylvie Ketchum was dead. Kim had decided that a long time ago. It was easier that way.

But just suppose…suppose her mother walked into the room right now, this minute. What would she say to Kim? What would Kim say to her?

"Sometimes I forget Dad isn't as young as he used to be," Kim told Wade now to explain Hugo's stepping back from Atlanta.

"Fifty isn't old," Wade argued.

"It isn't thirty, either." Or twenty, which was how old he had been when Sylvie had walked out on him.

"Maybe he's just tired," Wade said. "You have to admit he's been under a lot of pressure this past year. Justin didn't start out the season very well, then your illness. Once he takes this break, he'll be back with a vengeance, and everything will go back to normal."

She hoped Wade was right.

CHAPTER EIGHTEEN

THURSDAY MORNING Wade was standing in the middle of the central bay of the Fulcrum Motors garage area, surrounded by what might appear to an outsider as sheer chaos. Wade thrived on the challenge of bringing order to the seeming madness. He'd learned during his stints as acting crew chief to appreciate Hugo's extraordinary skill in orchestrating these weekly deployments to various tracks throughout the country. He had seen Kim's father on innumerable occasions standing in that very spot or leaning casually against a wall, coffee mug in hand, talking casually with people while giving directions, answering questions, helping people to organize or position things. No sweat. No strain. He made it all look so easy. It sure wasn't.

The wrong answer to a seemingly innocuous question could result in pieces of equipment having to be unloaded and the process started all over again. So far Wade had avoided that catastrophe, but the danger was ever present and kept him on his toes. He loved it.

The situation in Atlanta was equally challenging. Lose the confidence of the team, Wade knew, and he might never be able to get it back.

Wade didn't want to repeat the mistake of the previous week, when Justin suggested one solution for a problem and his crew chief, Hugo, insisted on another. In that particular case Hugo had been wrong. Lesson learned.

"I'm tight," Justin complained on his second practice lap. That meant his front end felt light and unstable.

"What do you suggest?" Wade asked. There were a variety of options, ranging from changes in tire pressure to adjustments in the sway bar, shock absorbers or a combination of them all.

"You tell me!" Justin snapped. A moment later he said, "Steering feels stiff."

"We'll start with the sway bar," Wade declared, trying very much to sound confident and decisive. His solution worked, but other problems developed. As soon as one was resolved, another popped up. Each adjustment seemed to incrementally improve car handling, but by the end of their allotted practice time, Justin was still dissatisfied with the way the car handled the turns.

Back at the garage that evening, they continued to discuss adjustments and made a few minor ones. Hope for a good qualification time the next day ran high, but team self-confidence seemed to be headed in the other direction.

JUSTIN PLACED TWELFTH in his qualifying lap on Friday.

"Good job!" Rachel bubbled, as though he'd taken the pole. "I just got off the phone with Uncle Hugo. He said twelfth is not a problem. You started in fifteenth last time and took the checkered flag. You'll do it again."

Atlanta had been Justin's first win of the season, after coming in forty-first in California and being a DNF—Did Not Finish—in Las Vegas.

Justin was pleased with his uncle's confidence in him, but he couldn't help frowning. His sister had taken it upon herself in the past few days to act as a mediator between him and Hugo. Maybe it was the mothering instinct Hugo had alluded to coming out again. Whatever it was, he wished she'd just butt out.

Justin needed a win badly to make up for Martinsville.

He wasn't about to voice it, but he also needed his uncle there to help him.

HUGO FELT STRANGE being at home in Charlotte on a weekend during the racing season. He spent most of Saturday in his daughter's hospital room, talking on his cell phone with Wade in Atlanta. He was gratified that his protégé was seeking his advice and was more than happy to share his experiences and opinions with the guy running *his* team. It was frustrating, though, being in one place when his gut said he ought to be somewhere else.

He had stopped off at Sylvie's room twice during his comings and goings. Both times the TV had been tuned in to the NASCAR Nationwide Series race, the sound turned low. Both times he'd found her sound asleep. He hadn't disturbed her.

He and Kim had eaten lunch and dinner off trays in her room. Wade was right—the food wasn't bad, only unimaginative. He had accompanied her on her mandatory evening stroll down the hall and back. They were both in good spirits, at least until they returned to her room late Saturday afternoon. The prospect of being alone there for hours on end lowered her spirits.

She flipped through the TV channels, discovered nothing of interest and turned it off. "Have you found out who the donor is?" she asked casually as she returned to The Weather Channel and lowered the volume to a whisper.

He'd been wondering when she would finally get around to asking the question. The longer she postponed it, the more prominently it seemed to hang in the air between them. For more than a week he'd been trying to decide how he would break the news of her mother's return at the same time he wondered how she would react when he did.

"Yes." He settled into the low chair and crossed his legs.

Kim gaped at him and waited for him to elaborate. When he didn't, she was obliged to ask, "It's her, isn't it? My mother."

He looked directly at her. "Yes, Kim, it is."

Her pink complexion became a deeper shade. Her lips thinned. She stared at him. "Were you planning to tell me?" The question was controlled but accusatory.

"I was waiting for you to ask, waiting for you to show that you were ready for the answer."

"And if I hadn't asked?"

"I knew eventually you would." The flash of fire in her eyes told him she didn't like being predictable.

"You've seen her, talked to her?" She was fighting to keep her words neutral. He admired her for that, though he knew it wouldn't last.

He nodded again and gave her time to assimilate the information.

"Since you're here alone," she finally said, "and not conveying any messages, it's obvious she doesn't want to see me." There was no mistaking the pain in her voice now, as if she had been rejected again.

"She loves you very much, Kim. She always has."

Fury raged in his daughter's eyes, although she kept her voice down. He sensed it was on the verge of breaking. "Sure. That's why she abandoned me. That's why she isn't here now."

He'd never expected this to be easy. "She'll tell you, Kim, that she didn't abandon you. She left you with me."

Kim glared at him uncomprehendingly, angrily. Finally she said, "She's not going to tell me anything, Dad, because I'm not going to let her. I don't want to see her. Ever."

He knew it wasn't true. They wouldn't be having this conversation if it were. But he knew, too, that she had her pride. She didn't want to be the one begging for reconciliation or forgiveness, not that she'd done anything to forgive. Her mother had. Kim had no idea how much there was to forgive her for.

"She gave you her kidney, sweetheart," he reminded her sympathetically. "Doesn't that tell you she cares?"

"Cares?" Kim exploded. "Cares? I don't know what her game is, but she's thirty years too late. She didn't care when I cried myself to sleep every night."

Hugo rose from the chair and stepped over to the side of the bed, concerned about more than his daughter's physical well-being. Her emotional state was at risk. He reached for her hand. "Kim, please, don't—"

"How long have you known?" she asked, pulling back from his attempt to touch her. "How long have you been seeing each other?"

In other circumstances he might have smiled at the way she phrased it, making it sound like they were having a clandestine affair. "When we went to see Dr. Peterson to schedule the surgery, everybody stepped out of the examining room for a couple of minutes, leaving me alone long enough to sneak a look at the file he'd left on the desk. I found the name of the donor and went to see her that afternoon to thank her for saving your life. Your mother answered the door."

"My *mother*." Kim repeated the word as if trying it on for size. "Did you know it was her before you went there?"

"I'd considered the possibility, but I wasn't sure. That was one of the reasons I went—"

"Why did she come forward now?"

"She heard Justin's appeal at Talladega for a kidney donor with AB-negative blood."

"And that's why we're a perfect physical match," Kim said.

He nodded.

"You knew it was her last Monday—" Kim was fuming "—and you didn't tell me."

"What would your reaction have been if I had?"

She wanted to say she would have rejected the

offer, but they both knew it would have been at the price of her own death.

"I don't know," she said in a huff, her tone less combative. "I wouldn't have been happy about it."

"Which is why I didn't say anything," he explained. "I didn't want you going into surgery depressed and angry. This is such a happy event, Kim. You've been given a second chance for a normal life. That's all that matters."

She couldn't deny it. "You deceived me," she said, though the sting was missing from her complaint.

"I held back information you didn't need to know, information that would have harmed you. I won't apologize for that. If I had it to do over again, I would do the same thing."

"She doesn't want to see me, does she?"

"Do you want to see her?"

"Don't answer my question with a question!"

He reached again for her hand, and this time she let him have it, but she still refused to meet his eyes. "She doesn't think she has a right to see you, Kim. She loves you, but she also knows how much she's hurt you."

"Well, I don't want to see her, either," Kim repeated like the frightened little girl she had been and maybe still was.

A minute slipped by in silence.

"Do the others know?" Kim asked. "Rachel and Justin? Do they know?"

"I haven't told anyone. Not even Dr. Peterson. There are only three of us who know. You. Me. And your mother." He saw her flinch again at the term. "I know this all comes as a shock—"

Kim snorted bitterly. "Shock? You must be kidding. No, Dad, it's not a shock. The shock was when I woke up from my nap and found my mother had deserted me. Everything after that is an anticlimax." Her face became a fixed mask. "You can give her a message from me, Dad. Tell her to go to hell!"

"Honey—" he squeezed her hand "—it wasn't like you think. She wasn't running away from you."

Should he tell her the whole sordid tale now? Was she ready to hear it? Would it bring Sylvie forgiveness?

"I'm tired, Dad. I think I'll ask the nurse for a sleeping pill and call it a night. If you don't mind…"

"I understand. Tomorrow we can talk about this again."

Tomorrow. Would Sylvie still be here tomorrow? Or would she have slipped out during the night? And when he told his daughter the story of her mother's ordeal, would Kim be able to appreciate Sylvie's dilemma and forgive her?

CHAPTER NINETEEN

NOTHING WAS GOING right.

Justin had placed twelfth in his qualifying lap on Friday. Not great, but Wade figured it wasn't all that bad. Two of the drivers in the top ten were rookies, a third was only in his second year at the NASCAR Sprint Cup Series level, and there were rumors he wouldn't be given a third. The driver in seventh place was a veteran, but his record this season wasn't impressive, either. He'd changed both cars and teams. So far his best showing had been fifteenth. Four drivers Wade figured Justin wouldn't have too much trouble putting in his rearview mirror.

The real challengers, in addition to Will Branch and Rafael O'Bryan, were Dean Grosso, Sophia's father, and Kent Grosso, her brother.

Justin had won Atlanta in March, beating out Dean Grosso by inches, while leaving Kent a dozen cars behind.

"You can do this," Sophia told Justin Sunday morning.

He kissed her hard. She was in a real spot. By cheering for her boyfriend, she was rooting against her own family, and family loyalty was important in the Grosso clan, especially against a Murphy.

"Just don't get cocky," Rachel warned him. "You've also got Will Branch and Rafael O'Bryan to contend with. Don't underestimate them."

Justin quickly moved from twelfth to ninth place, got drafted out by a trio and ended up back in twelfth place again.

"Pit stop," Wade told him.

"How many laps has it been?"

"Eighty-seven."

He should be good for a hundred, especially since he hadn't been in any crashes or near crashes, but Wade wanted to avoid what had happened at Martinsville. The trouble was that if Justin came in early, when he didn't need to, he might end up needing an extra pit stop, and that would cost him dearly in time. Still, an extra stop would be cheaper than running out of gas.

"Can we stretch it?" Justin asked, clearly trying not to sound as if he was challenging his crew chief.

"Three or four laps max," Wade answered, "and hope for a caution."

The yellow flag would freeze everyone in place

at a snail's pace, making a pit stop not nearly as costly, especially since most of the other drivers would be taking advantage of it, as well.

No caution. Justin came in. The stop lasted fifteen and a half seconds, at least a second and a half too long. He had just returned to the track when there was an accident coming out of Turn Two and the caution flag went up. Everybody went into slow motion. He burned gas for eight laps and gained nothing. That meant his next pit stop might have to be early, too.

In lap 156, Justin had a blowout.

In lap 198, he was sideswiped by Jem Nordstrom and ended up stalled in the infield.

By lap 300, he was barely holding on to thirtieth place and a lap down.

Another fifteen-plus-second pit stop.

"Come on, folks," Justin coaxed, reentering the track. He was two laps down now. "We've got to do better than this."

Three additional caution flags froze a total of seventeen unproductive laps. More gas was burned, but then, Justin reminded himself, so was everybody else's.

Justin maneuvered himself so that he was the first car a lap down. If there was another caution, the Lucky Dog rule would move him to the back of the lead lap, thereby gaining back his lost lap.

Not this time. Justin slipped back a little to where

he was directly behind the first car that was a lap down, getting ready to offer him a draft, when the next caution flag went up.

On lap 410 he got caught in an accident. His right front fender was damaged, his left rear panel nearly torn off. On pit road the crew was able to pound, pull and pummel the necessary pieces back into place. At least Justin wouldn't be a DNF, but his chances of finishing anywhere close to the front of the lead lap were as smashed as his grill.

"Hold your ground," Wade told Justin, as he re-entered the track for the last time. In other words, play it safe.

He did and finished in thirty-fourth place.

"KIM, WHAT'S the matter?" Rachel asked Monday morning. "Aren't you feeling well?"

She hoped, prayed her cousin wasn't having a setback. When she'd talked to her uncle yesterday afternoon following the Atlanta race, he'd reported that Kim was making excellent progress. Surely he would have called her and Justin if anything had changed.

"I'm okay." Kim made an effort to smile, but she wasn't very successful. "They're not sticking me with needles quite as often as they were, and the doctor says the tests all look good—"

"Then why are you so glum?"

"The race, right?" Justin asked. He was standing next to his sister. "I admit yesterday wasn't one of my better days."

Everybody was disheartened about Atlanta. It had been one of those races Rachel would just love to erase from her memory. If Kim was worried about what effect it would have on Wade's future career, she needn't have been. Justin could have shoved a large part of the disaster off on him. Pit-stop times had been the overall worst of the season, and there was good reason to question the crew chief's judgment regarding their timing, as well as his decision to change only two tires, instead of four, in the pit stop just before Justin had blown one of the unchanged tires.

But Wade hadn't been the only one at fault. The car's performance hadn't been all that great, which was Rachel's responsibility, and Justin's spotter had missed two excellent opportunities for him to move up early in the race when he was still in the lead pack. All in all just about everybody had screwed up in one way or another. The inevitable conclusion that none of it would have happened if Hugo had been in charge was pervasive, if not stated in so many words.

"Next week in Texas will be better," Justin promised, trying to sound upbeat. "You'll see."

Rachel was about to point out that it would be true

only if their uncle came back, but that would be an implied criticism of Wade, and she didn't want to hurt Kim that way. Besides, she suspected the race wasn't what was bothering her cousin. They'd all seen too many of them to allow one poor showing to break their spirits.

"What is it, Kim?" she asked again.

Her cousin nervously removed a piece of lint from her nightgown—gone were the ugly hospital gowns. "I had a talk with Dad Saturday afternoon," she muttered. "He knows who donated my kidney."

Rachel glanced over at her brother. His raised brow told her he was thinking the same thing she was.

"And?" Rachel prompted.

"My mother."

"She's alive?" Justin blurted. "I mean, we always figured she must be dead."

"Justin, why don't you sit down there—" Rachel indicated the chair by the window "—and shut up."

He ignored her.

Rachel kept her attention on her cousin. "He's been in contact with her? How long?"

"Since I was scheduled for surgery."

"And he didn't tell you until Saturday? Why?"

"She doesn't want to see me."

Rachel had to be careful not to overreact, but she couldn't remain passive, either. "She was willing to give you her kidney, but she doesn't want to see you? That's ridiculous."

"No," Justin interjected. "It's much easier to give a kidney anonymously than explain a thirty-year absence."

Rachel gazed pensively at him. "You may have a point." She turned back to Kim. "Do *you* want to meet *her?*"

"No." The answer came too quickly and too emphatically. "She doesn't want to see me, and I don't want to see her. We have nothing to say to each other."

The door opened. Everyone turned to see Hugo silhouetted against the light coming from the hall.

CHAPTER TWENTY

THREE PAIRS of eyes stared at him as he stepped into the room. No one greeted him. He let the wide door glide closed behind him.

"I told them," Kim announced in a tone that was somewhere between defiant and a pout.

He'd figured that out for himself.

"Was this the real reason you didn't want to go to Martinsville?" Justin asked. *Smart man.*

Hugo nodded. "Partly."

"Why didn't you just say so to begin with, instead of lying?"

"I didn't lie, Justin." He simply hadn't told the whole truth. What was it Sylvie had said, that equivocations were lies tied up in pretty ribbons?

"In retrospect, maybe I should have," he admitted. "It might have been easier for all of us, but I was afraid if I did, you would want to confront her, and she would flee. Where would Kim have been then?"

Thirty seconds went by before Rachel spoke up.

"She came this far after so long to give Kim her kidney. I can't imagine she'd be so cowardly that she'd turn around and leave without doing it, merely because someone yelled at her."

Hugo tilted his head. Leave it to Rachel to cut to the heart of the matter. "You're right, but I couldn't take that chance," he replied. "Given the situation, would you have?"

His niece considered the question a moment. "I guess not." Another beat of time passed. "What's she like? Did she tell you why she ran off? Where she's been all this time?"

What's she like? Did he really know? Were Rachel and Justin ready to hear the whole story, to learn the truth about their father? He'd palmed off a fantasy on them, that their daddy had been a handsome, dashing young race car driver who'd died in an unfortunate off-track accident. Would they believe him, and would they forgive him, if he told them now that their father had been an unprincipled lecher who'd been mowed down by one of his prey?

And what about Kim? Would she be able to understand what her mother had endured and forgive her for the terrible decision she'd made? More important, would she be able to cope with the knowledge that, in an effort to protect her, her mother had killed a man?

"I don't know all the places she's been," he acknowledged. "They're not important."

"So what happens now?" Justin asked.

"What do you *want* to happen?"

Kim shot him a furious look. He was answering a question with a question again. "I won't see her," she stated emphatically, "if that's what you're suggesting."

"She's planning to leave as soon as she's released from the hospital," Hugo said. "She could disappear again. She knows how. We may never get another chance to see her. You don't have to make up your minds this very minute, but there isn't a whole lot of time. I suggest you all think about it very carefully."

He gazed compassionately at his daughter. "You've waited thirty years to find her, Kim. I know this is very difficult for you, but please don't throw away this one opportunity. There may not be another. If nothing comes of it, so be it, but give yourself a chance to find out. I know you've got questions for her. Ask for the answers. I think you'll be surprised at how honest and forthright she'll be. No excuses. Just the truth. You deserve that."

"I said I don't want to meet her," Kim stated. "And I won't." She was angry to the point of tears.

"I won't, either," Rachel voted.

"Then it's unanimous," Justin concluded.

"READY TO GO home?" Dr. Peterson asked from the foot of the bed. He was wearing a starched white coat, the curled black tubing of a stethoscope peeking out of his large right patch pocket. In his left hand he held a patient folder.

Sylvie put a smile on her face. "Yes, Doctor."

She wouldn't miss this sterile room. Or the food. Or being poked and prodded at all hours of the day and night. The staff had been friendly and professional; she had no complaints about any of them. Some of them she might even miss, but not for long. She was ready to get back to her own life, to solitude rather than isolation, to productivity rather than boredom.

Except, leaving here would mean never seeing Hugo again. She'd dreaded seeing him, and now she dreaded not seeing him.

And Kim. She hadn't really seen her, only through binoculars, but once she left this building she would also be saying goodbye to the possibility of ever meeting with her.

That was the way she'd wanted it, wasn't it?

She'd set out to give her daughter another chance at a normal life, and she'd accomplished that. There was nothing more to ask for. She could move on with the rest of her life, consoled that she'd done all she could for the little girl she'd never stopped loving.

The surgeon was saying something— "…all look good. The nephrologist will still have to sign off on your release, and he won't be in for a couple of hours. Once he does, your discharge papers will go through and you will be free to leave. Let's take one more look."

She allowed him to examine her again. She winced when he palpated the site of the incision, but she did her best not to make more of the tenderness than it deserved. He covered her again and backed away.

"I have to warn you," he said, "you'll be sore for a while. I'll give you a prescription for pain medication." He rattled off a list of symptoms to watch for, detailed which of them were perfectly normal, which might require intervention. "You'll receive a packet of information going over the things I've just talked about, so you don't have to worry about having forgotten anything. You're in excellent general health," he concluded with an encouraging smile, "so I don't anticipate complications. Do you have any questions?"

She had none. "Thank you, Doctor. I'm very grateful for everything."

His expression became uncharacteristically modest. "It's been my privilege. What you've done, Ms. Smith, is a wonderful and generous gift," he concluded. "And a true inspiration." They shook hands.

Not everyone would agree with you, she thought

as she watched him leave. She was looking forward to returning to her cabin in the western hills. At least she told herself she was. She'd planned to relocate again if Hugo had found her, but ultimately rejected the idea. Chances were he knew where she lived now. Finding her again wouldn't be as difficult as it had been thirty years ago, if he really wanted to, and at the moment she didn't have the energy—or the will—to truly disappear.

She was reviewing her travel plans when she heard a gentle tap on the door. It opened and Hugo stepped in.

"You're looking better today," he said as he came closer, almost as if he was going to kiss her.

"I feel fine," she said. "But I can't say the same about you. Have you slept at all?"

He sauntered over to the chair by the window and settled wearily into it. "I've come to make a confession."

Under other circumstances she might have been tempted to tease him about his seriousness, ask him who he'd killed or what bank he'd robbed, but nothing about him invited humor. She was reminded again of how much she'd taken from this man.

"Confession of what?" she asked, matching his seriousness.

"I've told Kim you're here."

The words took her breath away. She closed her eyes, opened them.

"Oh, Hugo, you promised." She should be angry, but she realized she wasn't. On the contrary, it was as if a weight that had been pressing against her rib cage had suddenly been lifted. Her heartbeat raced.

Kim knows.

Why did it make her feel…happy?

"I'm disappointed in you." Was that true? Was she disappointed or relieved?

Hugo seemed so dejected she felt sorry for him. He was trying to do what was right. More than that, she realized, he was doing exactly what she had been secretly hoping he would do. But she couldn't tell him that. The situation hadn't changed. Nothing had changed.

He rose to his feet and approached the side of her bed.

"Come meet her, Sylvie," he pleaded. "Come see your daughter."

She studied him, pondered the beseeching expression in his eyes. It was tempting, oh, so tempting. Kim.

Then another truth revealed itself to her. Kim knew she was here, but she hadn't turned up with her father. Her daughter had refused to see her.

No more games.

"I'm being discharged today, Hugo," Sylvie

declared, and saw panic in his eyes. "I'll make a deal with you. The doctor tells me it'll be a couple of hours before the paperwork comes through and they officially release me." She waved to the clock on the wall. "I promise not to leave here for at least two hours, even if the paperwork arrives early. If Kim wants to see me, I'll be here. The choice is hers."

CHAPTER TWENTY-ONE

HAVING SEEN HER through binoculars at Martinsville, Sylvie shouldn't have been stunned by the sight of her daughter in the doorway—but there were fewer than ten feet separating them now.

"Kimmy," she whispered to the apparition standing before her.

"May I come in?" It was only then that Sylvie realized she'd never heard her grown daughter's voice. A mellow soprano. A comfortable sound, even if at the moment the tone was hesitant, verging on the confrontational.

"Of course. Here, take this seat." Sylvie motioned toward the chair closest to her visitor, while she herself instinctively leaned against the side of the bed where she'd placed her toiletries in preparation for packing them. Nearly two hours had gone by since Hugo had left. Sylvie had convinced herself her daughter wasn't coming. Then suddenly, there she was.

Sylvie's heart began pounding painfully. She

should sit, too. Her knees felt rubbery. She'd been experiencing weakness the whole time she'd been packing, her body still not back to its normal strength, but lounging in an armchair didn't seem appropriate, especially since Kim hadn't made a move toward the proffered seat.

"Your father tells me you're recovering very well. I'm so glad. Are the antirejection drugs terrible? I understand they can have very uncomfortable side effects. It might take a while to get them balanced." She was babbling. A discussion of rejection drugs was not why Kim was here. But she was afraid if she didn't keep talking, the apparition would disappear.

"They're all right," Kim replied without emotion. Her eyes hadn't strayed from her mother's. Sylvie was beginning to feel like a specimen in a dish. In a sense, she supposed she was. She couldn't expect a tearful hug.

Say something, girl. Yell at me. Curse me. Let me know I'm here, that I mean something to you. Anything.

"I understand you're engaged to be married," Sylvie finally said to break the tortured silence.

"Yes."

"I'm very happy for you and wish you all the best. Your father says he's a good man."

"He is."

Sylvie was beginning to feel dizzy. No wonder,

after all these years. She hadn't pictured their reunion being like this, but then, what else did she deserve?

"Do you mind if I sit down?" she asked. "I've been packing, as you can see—" she waved her arm toward the few belongings she had started shoving into the small valise she'd brought with her "—and I suppose that's the most exercise I've had in the past week. Too much lying around, I guess." She tried to smile, but the muscles of her face refused to cooperate.

Dr. Peterson had been right about the incision hurting. The excitement of seeing her daughter was exacerbating the tenderness, making it throb, turning the discomfort into pain. A small price to pay, she decided. Nevertheless, she reached for the arm of the chair and eased herself into it.

"Please sit down, Kim," she said, looking up at the slender woman in the satiny green dressing gown. "I know you have a mountain of questions. Ask them. I promise to answer every one of them truthfully and honestly. I won't hold anything back."

Kim stared at her a minute, then with seeming reluctance took the matching metal-frame chair. In spite of the frown pinching the corners of her mouth, there was a flare of vitality about her. Sylvie hoped it was because of the successful surgery, the new hope that her life could return physically to normal.

"Why did you abandon me?" Kim demanded. She

swept her hand through her shoulder-length auburn hair, not so much setting it in place as tugging at it. "Do you have any idea how many nights I cried myself to sleep, waiting for you to come home, wondering what I had done to make you not want me anymore?"

Maybe as many as I've cried, wanting to be there. You undoubtedly stopped crying. I never have.

"I'm sorry, Kimmy—"

"Don't call me that," her daughter said as if the familiarity was unwarranted. Maybe it was. "My name is Kim."

"I'm sorry, so sorry." Sylvie paused. "You didn't do anything wrong, Kim. You never did. You were the most precious thing in the world to me."

"Then why did you throw me away?"

"Oh, Kimmy—Kim, I didn't throw you away!" Sylvie cried in self-defense and shame. "I left you with Hugo because I knew you'd be safe with him. I was right, wasn't I? He's been a good father, a good daddy."

"I needed a mother, too. But you weren't there. What was I supposed to think?" Hand through the hair again, but this time Sylvie could see the hand was shaking. "Hugo once told me that maybe you were overwhelmed by having to bring up three kids, me and my cousins. Is that true?"

Sylvie nodded. "That's true, but it's not the entire reason. The situation was complicated." Instinctively she wanted to hold back, not talk about the events she'd relived in her mind, in her nightmares, so many times. But she'd promised her daughter honesty and candor. This might be the only opportunity she'd ever get to explain. If only this pain would go away.

"Your uncle, Hugo's brother, Troy, attacked me. It had happened before, and I wasn't going to let it happen again. This was after Ginny, Troy's wife, had killed herself with an overdose of sleeping pills."

Kim was staring at her, clearly not buying what she was hearing. What had Hugo told her and her cousins about Troy? That he'd been a good man who'd brought Hugo up single-handedly after their parents had died? It would be just like Hugo to recount only the good parts, ignoring the bad, especially since he was in denial about his brother's flaws.

"I managed to beat Troy off," Sylvie continued, "but he threatened to hurt not just me but you if I didn't give him what he wanted."

Perhaps that's what I should have done, given him what he wanted. Nothing would have been the same afterward, of course. I would have lost Hugo, but I could have kept Kim, and Troy would still be alive—until somebody else murdered him. At least I wouldn't be a killer.

"The night he died," Sylvie went on when Kim refused to react or comment, "I had driven into town to pick up the mail at the post office. It was raining. Troy came out of a tavern down the street. I wanted to scare him, to let him know I wouldn't let him threaten me or you. I didn't mean to hit him, but I did…and he died."

"You killed Uncle Troy?" Kim stared at her, her mouth hanging open.

Sylvie nodded. "I swear I didn't mean to. It was an accident, but I knew if I was caught, no one would believe me. Then Hugo asked me to help him raise Rachel and Justin. They were beautiful, delightful children, but every time I looked at them I was reminded that I'd killed their father. An accident. But that didn't matter. I was responsible for making them orphans, and I was positive that at any moment the police would come and arrest me."

Her heart beat faster as she recounted the events that had taken one life and ruined so many others. The pain in her side intensified.

"And so you left me without a word," Kim accused her.

"I was nearly insane with guilt and fear," Sylvie tried to explain. "I jumped at every sound, every creak of the trailer we lived in. A knock on the door had my heart in my mouth. I couldn't breathe. I couldn't eat. I couldn't sleep. I had to get away or I would go completely insane."

"Why didn't you take me with you?"

"I couldn't, sweetheart. I had no idea where I was going or how I was going to live. I had no education, no money, no prospects. No family worth mentioning. In fact, the vagabond life I led for the next five years was literally hand-to-mouth. Leaving you behind was the hardest thing I've ever done in my life, but it was the right thing. It was the right thing for you."

"Abandoning me, leaving me behind was the right thing?" Kim erupted. "I *waited* for you. Did you know that? I waited for years."

Sylvie lowered her head, unable to face her daughter, not wanting to picture her suffering, longing. How many times had she started back?

"Every night and every day," Kim said tightly, "I prayed for you to come home. But you never did."

"I never stopped loving you," Sylvie murmured, and lost her battle with tears. They rolled down her cheeks. She ignored them.

"But I stopped loving *you*," Kim declared coldly, as she rose to her feet.

"Don't go." Sylvie's head shot up. Panic raced through her. "Please. Stay a little longer. There's still so much to talk about, so much I want to say to you."

Kim stepped toward the door, stopped and turned around. "Thank you for giving me your kidney," she said in a voice that for the first time sounded compassionate. "I really am grateful to you for that. I won't say it's too little too late. You've saved my life, and for that I'll always be grateful." She returned to the chair she'd vacated, but instead of sitting in it, she gripped its back and continued to stand. "As for the rest…I don't know what to say, what to make of it."

"It's all true."

"It's incredible. Does Dad know you killed Uncle Troy?"

"Yes," Sylvie mumbled through a sniffle.

Kim shook her head in disbelieving wonder. "You killed his brother. You ruined my childhood…." She started to turn again and once more she stopped. "You didn't want to meet me, and when I found out you were here, I didn't want to meet you, either. Maybe we should have left it that way. Good luck with the rest of your life, but I never want to see you again. Not ever."

"Kim…"

The plea was lost as the door clicked firmly closed behind her daughter.

HUGO WAITED in the hall, not sure what to expect from the meeting between mother and daughter. Convincing Kim to take the first step, to break the impasse, hadn't been easy. If there had been more time he was certain he could have done a better job of it, but Sylvie was due to be discharged that afternoon. Once she went through the front door, he was convinced there wouldn't be a second chance.

He'd wanted to go in with Kim, to be by her side, to help them both cope with the painful awkwardness, but Kim had insisted on meeting her mother alone. He hadn't been sure it was a good idea. Having a third person present during such an emotional encounter often kept the two parties from saying things that were best left unsaid, at least initially.

Kim stepped out of the room, carefully closing the door behind her. She was trying to act cool, unshaken. She'd learned as a child to mask her emotions, and she was doing a masterly job of it now, but she couldn't fool her father.

"Well, that's done," she said with a casual sigh of relief, as if the encounter was nothing more than completing another medical form.

He didn't like the sound of it. "What did you talk about?"

Kim shrugged as they moved leisurely down the corridor toward the elevator. "She told me why she left. Very imaginative, I must say. I told her how much I'd missed her. End of story."

Not likely, he thought. "Are the two of you going to meet again?"

"No need. We each have our own lives to live

now. I thanked her for the kidney, told her I was very grateful."

And what else did you tell her? he wanted to ask.

"She made some really wild accusations, Dad. The woman is certifiable. Was she always that way, or was she just a little bit crazy back then?"

"She's not crazy, Kim."

His daughter ignored what he said as she repeatedly pressed the up button for the elevator. "She told me she's the one who ran down Uncle Troy. Can you imagine? She also said you knew about it."

"Not until recently. I only found out last week."

Kim turned to face him, her eyes wide. "You *believe* her? It doesn't bother you that she claims to have killed your brother?"

Where was this cold interrogator coming from? He'd known his daughter to be aloof, but not unfeeling. Then he realized that was precisely the point. She was feeling so much so deeply at the moment that she was projecting a facade of indifference to keep it all together. Should he leave her alone to have the breakdown he knew had to be coming? Should he call Rachel or Wade to be with her? Either way he didn't think he was the person to hold her hand right now. As far as she was concerned, he was part of the problem. He hoped he would be able to change that. Losing these two women in his life would be more than he could bear.

"Dad?"

"Uh-huh?"

Kim looked at him with concern. "I asked you if it doesn't bother you that she killed your brother."

"Of course it does!" he snapped. "But I also understand the circumstances. Did she tell you that he tried to force himself on her? That he threatened to hurt you? That she didn't mean to kill him? That she didn't even mean to hit him, just scare him?"

Kim's jaw had dropped. "You believe all that?" she asked incredulously.

The elevator arrived.

"I believe her."

He blocked the door from closing while standing back to let her enter first. They rode up in strained silence. He held the door for her again, but this time didn't follow.

"Give Rachel and Justin a call and ask them to join us in your room as soon as possible," he said. "It's time I explained a few things to all of you."

She gazed thoughtfully at him, then nodded. "I think you're right."

He pressed the button. The door slid shut. He faced the shiny panel for a moment, waited for it to reopen, then he retraced his steps to Sylvie's room. The first meeting between mother and daughter had obviously not gone well, but maybe it was enough for him to convince Sylvie to keep in touch. Maybe they would never be reconciled, but he had to do whatever he could to give them the opportunity to find peace with each other.

Regardless of Kim's attitude, he also knew he wasn't ready to say goodbye to the woman he'd married, the only woman he'd ever loved.

He tapped on the door, heard no reply. Surely she hadn't had time to sneak out yet. She could have taken the staff elevator down when they weren't looking, he supposed.

Ridiculous. He was being paranoid. Maybe she was in the bathroom.

He pushed the door release and stepped inside.

Sylvie was lying on the floor at the foot of the bed, not moving.

CHAPTER TWENTY-TWO

HUGO RACED through the doorway and fell to his knees, calling out Sylvie's name. She was pale as death. The thought rammed a cold shaft of steel down his spine. He placed two fingers on the side of her neck and felt for a pulse, but could detect nothing. Because he was so nervous or because there wasn't one?

He sprang to his feet, lurched to the emergency pull cord at the head of the bed, yanked it, then raced to the open door and called at the top of his lungs. "Help! I need help!"

A nurse appeared in the middle of the long corridor and ran toward him.

"She's unconscious," he said as the woman approached.

The nurse flew past him, sticking her stethoscope in her ears as she moved. She crouched by the prostrate patient, listened for a heartbeat and popped to her feet again. She was reaching for the phone when an aide stuck her head in the doorway, her face an open question.

"Call Dr. Peterson stat. Hurry."

"What is it?" Hugo asked from the corner where he'd retreated to get out of the way. "What's wrong with her?"

A male nurse materialized from nowhere, dropped to his knees and applied a blood-pressure cuff to Sylvie's left arm.

"Where's Peterson?" the first nurse barked.

"Right here." The surgeon hurried into the room, glanced for a microsecond at Hugo, then joined the others at the side of his patient. "What have we got?" he demanded without looking at his colleagues.

"Blood pressure forty-eight over zero and falling," the male nurse reported.

"Pulse 165 and thready," the female nurse added.

Peterson pulled away Sylvie's nightgown. The area of her incision was raised, red. It looked taut and tender.

An orderly wheeled a gurney into the room.

"What's happening?" Hugo begged again. "Is she going to be all right?"

"Set up an IV," the surgeon ordered. "I want a CAT scan stat. Call upstairs to the OR, tell them we have a bleeder and need a table ASAP. Check with the blood bank for her type, AB negative. We'll need at least two units, maybe three."

A bleeder. Hugo knew what that meant. Sylvie was hemorrhaging internally. She was bleeding to death without spilling a drop of blood.

He stood by, watching in helpless horror as Sylvie's limp body was hoisted onto the gurney in one deft motion by the male nurse and orderly. Immediately she was wheeled out of the room and to the right, followed nearly at a run by Dr. Peterson and the female nurse. Just before the nurses' station they turned sharply left and entered a long, wide staff elevator. The second nurse pulled Hugo back when he tried to enter with them. The doors closed. Hugo lurched forward as if to stop them.

"Wait here," the man commanded. "She's in good hands. There's nothing you can do."

The definition of helplessness. *Nothing you can do.*

HUGO LEFT WORD at the nurses' station that it was imperative he talk to Dr. Peterson as soon as the surgeon was available. He left Kim's room number, but made it clear he would meet the physician whenever and wherever he wanted. He suspected the doctor would be seeking him out, even without the prompting.

"What the hell's going on, Uncle Hugo?" Justin demanded the moment Hugo reached his daughter's room. "Kim just told us some fantastic story about her mother—"

"Sit down," Hugo said flatly.

Justin froze at the tone, then guardedly complied. Rachel, too, sank into a chair, her face questioning.

Hugo gazed at his daughter, sitting on the bed. She was confused, hurt and angry, and, he suspected, feeling guilty about her encounter with the woman she'd longed to love and now found she couldn't.

"Kim, honey, your mother collapsed right after you left her. I found her unconscious on the floor of her room."

Kim's whole body went still, her eyes wide. "Oh, my God!" she exclaimed, then covered her face with both hands.

Rachel jumped to her feet and went toward her, but Hugo was already there, putting his arms around her.

"How serious is it?" Rachel asked as Kim sobbed against his chest.

"I don't know. From what I was able to gather, she's bleeding internally. Fortunately Dr. Peterson was on the ward when I called for help. They've taken her back to surgery. I've left word—"

"It's my fault," Kim sobbed against his shirt.

"No, it isn't, sweetheart. Nothing you said could have caused her to hemorrhage. Don't even think it."

"You don't understand, Dad." Kim pulled away and looked at him with tear-drenched eyes. "She asked me if she could sit down." Kim grabbed a tissue. "She was weak and hurting, and I didn't even notice, because I was so angry at her, so bitter. I was thinking only about myself, not about her and what she must be going through."

"You had no way of knowing what her normal condition was." He tried to console her.

"I should have been able to see she was in pain. We'd both been cut the same way. I should have been more sensitive."

"Like I should have been when we were married. We see what we want to see, honey, and ignore things that don't fit our mental image. It's a natural human failing."

"It's not right," Kim said through her tears. "If you hadn't found her…" She paused. "Do you think she'll be all right?"

He wished he could give her the unequivocally positive response she was asking for.

"I don't know," he answered honestly. What he'd heard hadn't sounded very good. "In the meantime…we need to talk, get some things out in the open."

Deep inside, Hugo had always known this moment would come. He should be prepared with a smooth account of what had transpired, but maybe that wasn't possible.

He focused his attention on his daughter. "First of all, Kim, I want you to know that your mother didn't leave because she didn't love you. Don't ever think that, because it's not true."

He took a deep breath. "Let's start at the beginning. I know you've heard some of this before, but…" He let the sentence trail off. "Sylvie Ketchum was a country girl, smart but uneducated and naive as far as town and city living were concerned. She was fifteen when you were born, Kim, a single mother, living with her parents. She wasn't happy there, so she came here to Charlotte. I met her at the track."

"She and my father—" Kim paused, swallowed "—were they married?"

He'd told her her father had died in an accident, which was what Sylvie had told him. Had Sylvie said they were married, or had he assumed it? Either way, he knew differently now.

"No." He watched his daughter, saw that the news came as a disappointment but no great shock. He had to wonder how long she'd been harboring doubts about her own legitimacy. "Which was one reason Sylvie decided to leave home. The community where she lived…well, social attitudes were different back then."

"You also told me my father was dead. Was that a lie, too?" she asked, a note of accusation creeping into her voice.

"I didn't lie to you, Kim. I told you what I thought was true at the time. It was only this past week I learned otherwise. As for your father, yes, he's dead. He died before you were born."

"He forced himself on her, didn't he?" Kim whispered, and hung her head. "My father forced my mother to—"

"Yes," Hugo said softly.

Without looking at him, Kim gave a slight nod.

"The rest of what I have to tell you isn't pleasant, either. For any of you. That's why I've never told you about it, but the time has come—"

"Yes, it's time we knew," Justin said, the fire of his earlier contentiousness gone.

Rachel nodded her agreement.

Hugo paused, wondering if he was doing the right thing. Taking another deep breath, he began.

"My brother, Troy, was a man of contradictions. Smart, fun-loving and charismatic, as I've told you. He took care of me after our parents were killed in a car accident and always made sure I did my best. I'll always be grateful to him for that. What I didn't tell you was that he was also self-absorbed and abusive." He shifted his attention between Rachel and her brother. "Your mother—Virginia, Ginny—was like Sylvie in many ways, an unsophisticated country girl. Your father got her pregnant and did what was considered the right thing back then. He married her. Suddenly Ginny found herself out of her depth. It all got to be too much for her. One day she took a bottle of sleeping pills."

"When I was two," Rachel noted. "And Justin was less than a year old."

Hugo nodded. "She was overwhelmed by everything going on around her, sweetheart. Nowadays we would call it postpartum depression. Back then we knew nothing about the syndrome, didn't even have a term for it, except maybe moody. My brother, I'm sorry to say, was no help. Actually, he was a large part of the problem. He was arrogant, demanding, unsympathetic and a notorious womanizer who made no secret of the fact that he was playing around with other women. It's taken me this long to realize how completely insensitive he was, insensitive and even cruel."

"What's that got to do with my *mother* leaving?" Kim asked, as if the word didn't quite fit her tongue. But Hugo sensed dread in her tone, as well. Sylvie had already told her what she had done, and now he was about to confirm it.

"Troy bullied her," he said. "He showed every indication he was willing to force himself on her—"

"Whoa," Justin interrupted. "Are you telling us our father—"

Hugo gazed down at his hands. "Yes."

"Did you know about this?" Justin asked, obviously rocked by the revelation.

Hugo shook his head. "I had no idea until Sylvie told me about it last week."

"And you believe her? Why?" Justin demanded. "This is completely different from the picture you've always painted of our father."

"I wanted you to have a good image of your dad, but when Sylvie told me what happened, so many things began to make sense." Hugo looked from face to face, saw the bewilderment, the doubt.

"You can blame me for a lot of what happened," he went on. "Had I been more alert, more honest, more willing to open my eyes to the truth, things might have turned out differently." He pinched the bridge of his nose. "Here's what really happened."

He told them about the night of Troy's death. They looked at him in horror throughout his narrative. Except for Kim. She kept her head down and sniffled into a tissue.

"Let's see if I have this straight," Justin finally said, his voice softened now with compassion. "You're telling us that Kim's mother killed our father?"

"Not intentionally."

"Oh, my God!" Rachel exclaimed.

"So it's true." Kim raised her tearstained face. "What she said is true."

"It was an accident," Hugo reiterated. "A tragic accident."

"You're defending her?" Rachel sounded outraged.

"I'm saying I can understand how it happened…and why. It seems to me she's paid a pretty heavy price."

"By walking away with her freedom and leaving Kim behind?" Rachel asked.

Hugo momentarily closed his eyes and sucked in a breath. He'd hoped to gain sympathy for the woman he loved, but he was obviously not succeeding.

"Consider what would have happened if she'd stayed," he continued. "She'd been trying to protect Kim from a man who had threatened to harm her. She didn't intend to run your father down, but that's what happened. Maybe if he had been sober he would have reacted differently, but we'll never know that. The point is, she'd just caused her brother-in-law's death, then I asked her to bring up his children. She loved you, she truly did, but every time she looked at you she was reminded that she'd killed your dad, made you orphans, all of this on top of her constant fear that the police were going to arrest her at any moment."

"She killed a man," Justin said in a raised voice. "She killed my father. Damn right she deserved to be arrested."

"She wouldn't disagree with you, son, but think about it. Not only would she have been sent to prison, Kim would have been branded for the rest of her life as the daughter of a murderer."

A small moan escaped Kim.

Rachel reached forward and took Kim's hand in hers. "It's not your fault."

Justin rose, came over to the bed and put his arm around Kim's shoulders, as well. "What she did has nothing to do with you, Kim."

The confusion in his eyes returned as he addressed his uncle. "What I don't understand is why you would even want us to meet her. She killed our father, left you without a word of explanation and abandoned her child. Now, thirty years later, she returns and you want us to be all forgiving. Why?"

Hugo got to his feet and walked over to one of the windows and gazed out at the gray autumn sky and the traffic on the street below.

"Because I am responsible for what happened, too," he declared, and heard the words bounce off the hard, clear glass in front of him. Without turning to face them, he said slowly, "I had the power to stop him. I had the obligation to protect the people I loved, who depended on me, and I failed to do it."

He spun around and gazed at the three young people he'd dedicated his life to. "My brother hit on my wife, threatened her, and she was afraid to tell me because she didn't think I would believe her. The truth is she might have been right. Troy was a depraved son of a bitch, and I—" he felt his throat tighten, burn "—I was his enabler. Between us we drove a good woman to such desperation that she was forced to try—not very smartly, as it turned out—to protect her daughter from him. She ran away from me when she should have been able to run *to* me."

Overwhelmed with guilt and shame, he commanded himself to look directly at Kim. "She left you with me because she wanted to spare you the life she knew she would have to live, always looking over her shoulder, forever afraid. I can't give her back the thirty years she's lost, just as I can't give back to you all those years without a mother. What's lost can never be returned, but maybe a little understanding can make the loss more bearable."

Rachel whispered, "You're still in love with her, aren't you?"

Hugo looked up and gave the mother-to-be a wry smile. "Yes."

CHAPTER TWENTY-THREE

"DAD," KIM CALLED.

Hugo was staring out the window again, though he couldn't have said what he was seeing. He turned around. Kim was standing by the side of the bed, her eyes red and watery. She kept wringing her hands. Rachel and her brother had left a minute earlier to go down to the cafeteria with a promise to bring back sandwiches. No one had gotten around to lunch today, except Kim, who was still under strict orders to clean her plate.

"Thank you for being my father," she said quietly. "Mom was right. You've been a great dad. I couldn't have asked for better." She extended her arms.

He came forward then and held her. She clung to him more tightly than she had in years, and for a fleeting moment she was his little girl again.

"I love you, Dad."

"And I love you."

They held each other in silence. He realized tears

were rolling down his cheeks. They would get through this. Kim was on the road to recovery. He prayed Sylvie would be all right, too. Even if Kim didn't want her to be a part of her life, he wanted Sylvie to be a part of his. Somehow they would work it out. Sylvie had to stay, or he would have to leave.

"We need to check on Mom," Kim said.

Hugo stepped out of her embrace. "I'll go downstairs and see what I can find out."

But the nurses on the floor below couldn't tell him anything, except that they would pass on Hugo's request to see Dr. Peterson.

Rachel and Justin were back in Kim's room when Hugo returned. The sandwiches and salads they'd brought looked good, but no one did more than nibble at them. Hugo answered questions as honestly and completely as he could.

Two hours passed before there was a tap on the door. Dr. Peterson came into the room, wearing wrinkled green surgical scrubs now, looking wrung-out and none too pleased.

"Is she going to be all right?" Kim asked immediately.

Peterson ignored her and focused on Hugo. "How did you find out about her?" he demanded.

Hugo apologized and explained what he had done and why.

The surgeon gazed at his other patient. "Her daughter. I suspected you might be." The expression on his face wasn't particularly friendly. "It explains the perfect match. Nevertheless—" he glared at Hugo again "Ms. Smith requested anonymity as an organ donor, and I gave her my word she'd get it. Do you have any idea the position you've put me in? I could be brought up on ethics violations if she chooses to press the matter, and it could have a dire impact on the integrity of the entire organ-donor program."

Hugo again apologized. He had the impression the surgeon was more interested in making a point than he was seriously worried about the violation, for which Hugo was willing to take full responsibility.

"How is she, Doctor?" Kim asked again.

"Sorry, patient information is confidential."

"You can release it to family, can't you?" she snapped back angrily.

He hesitated. "Yes, but—"

"Then tell me," Kim demanded. "I'm her daughter."

Hugo's face broke into a wide, relieved smile. He clutched Kim's hand.

"Tell me about my mother, Doctor," she said. "Is she going to be all right or isn't she?"

Peterson was silent for a moment, his gaze taking in the family tableau, then he relaxed.

"Ms. Smith," he said, "was bleeding internally.

For how long, I'm unable to say, but by the time she collapsed, the hemorrhage had put her life in jeopardy. We've transfused her with three units of blood so far. The rupture has been repaired and the bleeding's stopped."

Kim closed her eyes and nodded gratefully.

"She's not out of the woods yet," the doctor warned. "We have her in ICU under close observation. At the first sign of any further internal bleeding, we may have to go in again. I hope that won't be necessary. Every incision exposes a patient to infection."

"Can she have visitors while she's in the ICU?" Kim asked.

The surgeon rubbed his forehead. "She stated in her medical history that she had no relatives and didn't want visitors. Under the circumstances—" he narrowed his eyes at Hugo "—since she has already made you an exception, I'll leave word that you and your daughter may be admitted to see her, separately, and only for a minute or two, until she wakes up and can decide for herself." He rose and left the room.

THE WOMAN IN THE BED looked smaller than the person Kim had met earlier that day. The salt-and-pepper hair was hidden under a cap. Her complexion, much paler than Kim remembered it, had a translucent quality.

An IV was securely taped to the back of Sylvie's left hand, but the right hand was free, and Kim grasped it greedily.

"Mom, it's Kimmy," she said in a soft whisper tinged with tears. "I'm here. Dad is outside, waiting to come in and tell you how much he loves you. I'm sorry for the way I treated you today. I didn't understand. I hope you'll forgive me. I've waited so long to see you—" tears ran down her face "—and when I finally did, I blew it. Dad has explained everything to me."

Kim studied her mother's face, searching for some sign of awareness. Did Sylvie know she was beautiful?

"Dad is scared you're going to leave him again. He still loves you, Mom. I guess he always has. I don't want you to leave again, either. I want you to stay. I want you to come to my wedding. I know it won't be easy for you, but you can count on Dad and me, and later on, Justin and Rachel, too."

A teardrop fell on the back of Kim's hand. She ignored it. "This has all been so unfair. All these years apart when we should have been together. I wish you hadn't left. I wish you could have taken me with you, but if you couldn't, I'm glad you left me with Hugo. You did the right thing in trusting him. No one could ask for a better dad."

A nurse came by and indicated with a tap on her watch that it was time to leave.

"I have to go now, Mom. But I won't be far away. Wake up soon. We have so much to talk about, so much to share." Kim rose, started to leave, then turned back. "I love you."

She squeezed her mother's hand, then left the room. Outside the ward Hugo and Wade were waiting for her, Hugo questioning her with his eyes.

She shook her head. "She's still asleep. I don't know if she heard me or not. Do you think she did?"

Wade wrapped his arms around her and hugged her gently.

"Yes, deep inside I think she heard you," he said. "She's your mother. She loves you. She always has. That counts for everything."

THE FOLLOWING MORNING Sylvie was moved from the ICU back to her private room. Kim and her father were there, Kim in a wheelchair, he sitting on the bench by the window, apparently lost in thought.

Sylvie's eyelids fluttered.

"She's coming to," Kim said in a low but excited voice. "Dad, she's waking up."

Kim locked the wheels of her chair, lifted the foot rests and stood up. Hugo, roused from his reverie, moved quickly to the other side of the bed. Each took one of Sylvie's hands.

Another minute elapsed before the woman in the bed completely opened her eyes. She appeared uncertain at first, disoriented, perhaps afraid.

"Hi," Hugo said with a warm smile. "Welcome back. How do you feel?"

She said nothing for a minute, as if weighing the question and her reply. "Confused, I guess." She gazed at Kim, then shifted her eyes to Hugo again. "Thirsty."

He picked up the oversize drinking mug and brought the flexible straw to her lips. "Slowly now."

She raised herself ever so slightly to sip, then collapsed back into the pillow. Another moment passed. Her eyes flicked from him to their daughter.

"What are you two doing here?"

"Mom, I'm sorry I was so mean to you. I was wrong. Very wrong. I hope you'll forgive me."

"It's me who needs forgiveness," Sylvie said, her voice rusty. "I never meant to hurt you. I just didn't—"

"Shh," Kim soothed. "I understand now. There's nothing to forgive."

"But—" Sylvie started to become restless.

"Easy, easy," Hugo said, placing a hand comfortingly on her shoulder. "Everything is going to be all right." He offered her another sip from the mug. She drank more greedily this time.

"I don't understand," Sylvie finally said. "Why are you here?"

"Because I'm your daughter, Mom," Kim said, and tried to smile. "And I want to be with you."

Sylvie wept, the tears running down the sides of her face. Kim handed her a tissue.

"Sorry, honey," Hugo said to her with a self-conscious grin, "time for poking and prodding. If I don't let them know you're awake, they'll have my hide." He pressed the call button and informed the voice that answered that Ms. Smith was awake.

Only seconds later, a nurse came in, greeted Sylvie like an old friend, applied a blood-pressure cuff, then clipped an oxygen reader to her right index finger. She checked the readouts. "Textbook perfect. I'll call Dr. Peterson and let him know. He'll be by to see you later." The nurse left.

"You think you're up to having more visitors?" Hugo asked Sylvie.

She gazed blankly at him, her mind apparently still not completely clear. "Who?"

"Rachel and Justin would like to meet you."

"Oh, Hugo, I don't know…."

Kim stroked her hand. "It's all right, Mom. I promise."

Sylvie focused on her daughter. After so many years she was being called Mom again. Sylvie didn't say anything, but she didn't have to. Kim smiled encouragingly and stroked her hand.

Hugo went to the door and beckoned the sister and brother in.

SYLVIE WATCHED them enter the room, Justin tall and strong, and for a moment frighteningly resembling his father. But Troy was long dead, and Sylvie knew from all the reports and articles she'd read that his son was a decent man. The sight of Rachel, on the other hand, brought a momentary wave of sadness. She looked remarkably like her mother, though Virginia hadn't lived as long as this young woman had. Ginny would have been proud of her children. Damn the man who had robbed her of that, of life itself. But she wasn't going to dwell on the past, on people who had long since gone to their graves. She had to face the living.

The two came shyly, hesitantly, up on Hugo's side of the bed.

"Hello, Sylvie," Justin said, taking the initiative. "You gave us a quite a scare there. I'm glad you pulled through all right."

"Thank you."

"You're every bit as beautiful as Uncle Hugo said you were," Rachel added.

Sylvie glanced at Hugo. "Beautiful?"

"You always were to me," he said.

She looked at Justin. "You have every right to hate me."

"For defending yourself and your daughter?" He shook his head. "I don't think so."

"Uncle Hugo says you want to leave," Rachel said. "I hope you don't. We'd like to get to know you better."

Sylvie took in the faces around her. They all seemed to be saying the same thing. *Stay.*

"I'm not sure I can," she said.

"Yeah, you can," Hugo assured her. "If you want to. I've talked to a lawyer, one I trust, and explained what happened. He's made some discreet inquiries. Troy's death was filed as a hit-and-run by person or persons unknown. No evidence was ever collected that could identify the culprit. The case was essentially closed thirty years ago. No one is interested in reopening it now, especially without any evidence. All they would have is your word that you were responsible. So—"

"If you keep quiet about it," Justin said, "we will."

"Even your confession isn't proof," Rachel added.

"A good lawyer would get it thrown out in a heartbeat," Hugo said.

"So there's no need for you to go anywhere, Mom," Kim told her. "You're home now. To stay."

EPILOGUE

"I FEEL LIKE I have a lead anchor dragging my right rear," Justin Murphy reported as he rounded Turn Four.

"I can't see anything wrong," his spotter reported from his roost above the grandstands. "No metal dragging."

"It's tight," Justin insisted. "Feels like a tire."

"Oh, I wish we could be there," Kim said, staring at the big plasma screen mounted on the wall in Hugo's den. "I miss the noise."

"I can turn up the volume," Sylvie offered. They were listening to a special feed of the Fulcrum team radio communications at Phoenix, while watching the race on TV.

"Not the same," Kim remarked. She was sitting beside her mother on the leather couch. Their incisions were healing nicely, according to Dr. Peterson. Not nearly fast enough, according to them.

"And what about the smells, the heat, the ground shaking?" Kim asked.

"It's okay." Sylvie reached over and clasped her daughter's hand and smiled happily. "There'll be plenty of other races. At least your father was able to get this intercom hookup, so we can eavesdrop on what's going on."

"Yeah, almost as good as being there," Kim remarked unconvincingly. Nothing compared to being at a NASCAR race.

But the two women were too recently out of surgery to be making cross-country plane trips to race tracks. They'd missed the competition in Texas last weekend—Justin had come in seventh—and now this race in the Valley of the Sun. They'd have to miss the season's climax at Miami-Homestead next weekend, too, although if Justin was able to win the checkered flag today and the right people did relatively poorly, his No. 448 might still have a chance in terms of points for the NASCAR Sprint Cup Series Championship—but only if he took the checkered flag there, too.

"A lot of *ifs,*" Kim reminded her mother, "but miracles do happen." Hadn't Hugo found Sylvie after thirty years? Hadn't she reconciled with her mother and the rest of the family?

If Justin did come in first today, Hugo had promised Kim he'd arrange for a special medical team to accompany them to Miami. Sylvie hadn't been reintroduced to the NASCAR world yet. Why not start at the final race of the NASCAR season?

"Let's go with two tires on the outside," they heard Hugo tell Justin. The intercom hummed with background noise. "We'll give you a splash at the same time."

"Smart move," Sylvie commented. "If the change does the trick, Justin should be able to finish the race without having to pit again."

They were down to the last forty laps of the 500-mile race. Justin had led six laps earlier in the race, then lost the advantage when he was obliged to come in early because of a traction-bar problem following a bump by Jem Nordstrom going into Turn Three. It was only because of Justin's skill as a driver that he'd avoided wiping out. Kim was proud of the way her cousin was handling himself, professionally and personally. After meeting Sylvie in her hospital room and spending several more hours talking with her privately later, he'd come to appreciate her situation, as well as his uncle's. Facing the unpleasant truth that the father he'd never met had been a loser on several levels hadn't been easy, but Justin had accepted it and convinced Rachel, as well.

While Justin swung onto pit road and jammed on his brakes to conform to the speed limit, Kim glanced over at her mother. Kim had taken her to her hairdresser, who'd turned plain to luxurious and drab into multihued shiny brilliance. Sylvie's wardrobe had undergone a metamorphosis, too. Not to anything flashy or chic, but to elegantly stylish.

Feeling remarkably contented with her life now, Kim tried to concentrate on what was happening on the screen. The crew had hung out the shingle with No. 448 and the Fulcrum colors emblazoned on it. Justin veered sharply to the left and skidded to a stop within the painted borders of his box. Two tires were changed. The tank was topped off, and the car was again on its way. The pit time was posted in the lower-left corner of the screen: 12.96.

"Not bad," Kim said approvingly. "Less than thirteen seconds. Not bad at all."

Justin burned rubber out of the pit box, weaved back and forth to heat up the new tires. At the end of pit road he mashed the gas pedal to the floor. Smoke puffed up, the rear end skidded and he shot directly into Turn Three.

He wove among the cars in the second pack.

"Will Branch is asking for a draft," his spotter informed Justin over the intercom.

Will was three laps down because of a blowout earlier in the race. Barring a pile-up that eliminated half the field, there wasn't enough time left for him to catch up, but a draft might allow him to gain a few positions and garner extra points.

"On my way," Justin shifted to the outside lane where Will was pacing Finnegan Jarvis but seemed unable to outgun him.

Justin nosed up onto Will's tail. Combining their airstreams decreased wind resistance, increasing the speed and fuel efficiency of both cars. A second later, virtually locked bumper-to-bumper, they began to move up as one. Will inched ahead of Jarvis and kept going, Justin on his tail.

They advanced on Nils Booker and passed him. Passed Barney Constantine and Mitch Volmer. Still drafting, with Will in the lead, the pair emerged in front of the trailing pack.

"Time to make your move," Kim muttered at the screen.

As if he'd heard her, Justin slingshotted left, took advantage of the momentum the draft had given him and pulled ahead of Will. He was in the lead of the trailing pack.

"Good move. Lucky Dog," Sylvie murmured. "Now let's hope for a yellow flag."

Kim glanced over at her mother and grinned. Sylvie knew the rules and the tactics in play here. The caution flag froze the field in slow motion and permitted drivers to make pit stops without giving up as many positions as they would have at competition speeds. The Lucky Dog rule allowed the lead car in the one-lap-down pack to advance to the end of the lead lap, essentially giving the driver a free lap. Justin was in that spot right now.

"Nordstrom is still in front, eight cars ahead of you," the spotter told Justin. "Dean Grosso is dogging him, but doesn't seem to have the juice to pass him."

The Phoenix track was a mile long and oddly shaped, not quite a standard D. But then, every NASCAR track was unique.

"Nordstrom is at least six laps late taking his last pit stop," Wade reminded driver and crew over the radio.

"He's running on fumes and praying for a caution flag," Sylvie remarked. No driver ever wanted to have to give up the lead for a pit stop, especially late in a race.

"He's pulling in," the spotter announced. "Nordstrom's on pit road. Dean has the lead."

"Uh-oh," Sylvie said. "Looks like we have—"

"Yellow flag! Yellow flag!" the spotter interrupted excitedly. "Constantine just clipped Volmer. We have an accident."

"And a Lucky Dog," Kim said, the satisfaction in her voice obvious.

Five laps later the green flag replaced the yellow. Justin now had advanced to the end of the lead pack, no longer a lap down. He had seven cars ahead of him in the lead pack and Nordstrom immediately behind him.

"Check Nordstrom," Hugo warned Justin. "Keep your eye on No. 486."

But something was wrong. Nordstrom not only didn't challenge Justin, he lost ground to three other cars. He'd changed four tires during his pit stop.

"He could be having trouble with the cold rubber," Hugo explained, "or he's developed engine trouble, or they made some adjustment that's backfired."

Twenty laps to go.

Justin pulled ahead of Bart Branch.

Slipped to the inside of Rafael O'Bryan.

Played cat-and-mouse for three laps with Haze Clifford. Nosed ahead of him going into Turn One.

Four laps to go. Only Crane Dawkins and Kent Grosso were ahead of him now.

Justin tried to maneuver around Dawkins, but the twenty-year veteran seemed to anticipate his every move and counter it. Flying down the backstretch, Justin was inching up on the inside lane when Dawkins lost his concentration for a split second, miscalculated where Justin was or had one of those momentary engine sputters.... Whatever it was, Justin's right fender made contact with Dawkins's left bumper, enough to destabilize Dawkins. Justin hugged the middle of the track and pulled ahead, as Dawkins careered into the wall.

"It's down to Justin and Kent Grosso," Kim said.

Weave and dart. Three laps to go.

"Come on, Justin." Sylvie clenched a fist. "Go for it."

Justin in the middle lane. Two laps to go.

Justin in the inside lane. The white flag. One lap to go.

Turn One. Side by side. Justin a bumper ahead.

"Yes!" Sylvie said, louder this time.

Turn Two. Side by side. Kent ahead by a few inches.

Backstretch. Justin on the inside. Kent crawling ahead on the outside.

"Go, go, go, go, go!" Kim screamed, springing to her feet.

Turn Three. Justin slightly ahead.

Sylvie was up beside her. "Yes! Go! Yes! Yes!"

Turn Four. Kent squeezing left against Justin.

"Come on! Come on!" Sylvie yelling wildly now.

Justin not yielding. Neck and neck, heading into the frontstretch.

Justin edged forward.

Sylvie pumped her right fist into the air. *"Yes!"*

The checkered flag waved. Justin won by inches.

KIM HAD SPOKEN with Wade on the phone. Sylvie had talked to Hugo. Both men promised to be home that night, but it would be after midnight. Both women promised to be waiting, no matter how late it was. Sylvie served beef pot pie that Kim said was to die for. They watched reruns of the day's race, listened to the pundits comment on the events and dozed. At 2:15 a.m., Hugo and Wade arrived. Within minutes Kim was beside Wade in his pickup heading "home."

Hugo and Sylvie sat on the butter-soft leather couch, holding hands, ignoring the forty-year-old Hollywood classic on the movie channel. He slipped his arm across her shoulders; she burrowed contentedly into his side.

He told her about his plans to get her and Kim to the race in Florida the following weekend. When she didn't respond, he leaned forward and turned to her.

"What are you thinking?" he asked, though he suspected he already knew.

"That I don't want to go. Well…I do. I want to be with you and Kim, but—"

"But you'll have to face people," he concluded. "You're brave enough to face anything, Sylvie."

"It's not me…not only me," she corrected. "I'll be an embarrassment to you and Kim, to Justin and Rachel. There will be so many questions. How do we…how do I answer them?"

"You had it right the first time, sweetheart. *We.* Seems to me a very wise person told me not too long ago that the time for lies and deceit are past. How about we just tell the truth—that you came back when you learned your daughter needed a kidney and you decided to stay."

She stared at him. "The media will want more."

True. If he could get the media to back off, to respect their privacy... But he was being naive. Privacy was a foreign concept to the media.

"I propose that we just say you're Mrs. Hugo Murphy," he said.

She laughed. "Hugo, I haven't been your wife in over twenty years. Don't you think they'll wonder where I've been?"

He adjusted his hold on her, enjoying the warmth of her body against his. "I didn't say ex-Mrs. Murphy. I said Mrs. Murphy. The current Mrs. Murphy."

She turned her head sharply, her eyes wide. "Hugo, you're not serious."

"I love you, Sylvie," he murmured in her ear and tightened his hold on her. He wasn't letting her go this time. "I know now I've always loved you. I failed you as a husband once—"

"No—"

"Let me finish. I failed you once, Sylvie, failed to protect you, to fully appreciate you. And now I'm asking you to give me another chance, a chance to be the husband you deserved back then and still deserve now. Please, marry me."

"Oh, Hugo." She threw herself against him. He closed his eyes and savored the sensation of her body pressed against him, but he was also aware that she hadn't said yes. He opened his eyes and gazed down at her.

"Will you, Sylvie? Will you marry me? I don't know exactly how we'll handle the press and the other people—the Grossos, in particular. But we'll weather the storm together. Justin and Sophia have proved that we don't have to be bound by the past, that the future can be different."

"You may regret this," she murmured against his chest.

Never. "Then you will? You'll marry me?"

"Yes, Hugo, I'll marry you. Again. You're the only man I've ever loved. The only man I ever will. Yes, I'll marry you and hope we have a bunch of grand-kids together!"

He kissed her hard. "I love you, Sylvie."

* * * * *

For more thrill-a-minute romances set against
the exciting backdrop of the NASCAR world,
don't miss EXTREME CAUTION
by Jean Brashear.
Available in December.
For a sneak peek, just turn the page!

"YOU'D THINK I WAS a teenager going out on her first date." Abruptly Maeve wished she hadn't used that word.

"This wasn't a date." Chuck's eyes gleamed even in the darkness. "When we have a date, you'll know it, Maeve."

His voice was a low caress that tugged at something deep in her belly. He took her hand. Brought it to his lips.

Made her shiver.

"I'm a patient man where you're concerned, Maeve. Surprises the hell out of me. I didn't make my fortune by being patient." He bent his head to hers, and she forgot how to breathe. "But you're worth waiting for." He brushed his lips over hers.

"I—" All her thoughts scrambled. She could still recall the feeling of having him stand between her and trouble tonight, shielding her as he had at La Mireille. He was a strong, confident man, but he'd also shown her gentleness. It would be easy, so very easy to lean.

She forced herself to sit up. Remove her hand from his. "I'm not ready," she managed, but her voice was still hoarse. Breathy.

His grin was wry. "I'm all too aware of that." He patted her hand once, then faced the front. "That's where the patience comes in."

"I might not ever be," she confessed. "You shouldn't wait on me."

His gaze was hard and predatory. "What I choose to do with my time is my decision." Then he glanced ahead. "Here we are."

Maeve grasped her purse and let the driver hand her out, then retrieve her suitcase. She followed Chuck to his plane, admiring the lines of it, understanding from her experience with other aircraft that his was top-notch.

This plane, like the man, was solid and strong and sure.

But she couldn't afford to get involved with a man like that. She needed to be that way herself. She was through being coddled, kept blind like a hawk being brought to hand by its owner, however much being on her own frightened her.

Were her boys right? Was she too old to find her own way? Had she been caged too long to fly free?

Her mind was spinning with questions and doubts, and a headache was brewing behind her eyes.

"Relax, Maeve. I'm not going to jump you just because I have you at my mercy."

She looked up as he stood over her. "I wasn't thinking any such thing."

He crouched beside her. "You're worrying about something, and you never answered me about whether you'd had dinner."

"I'm not hungry."

He glanced back at the attendant she hadn't noticed before. "A cup of tea—Earl Grey, I think—and some of those scones. I learned a taste for them when I visited Scotland." At her soft protest, he speared her with a glare. "If you want me to leave you alone, then prove to me you can at least take care of your health."

She frowned. "I'm not helpless."

"I never said you were. If you'll recall, I said you are one very brave woman." He leaned closer. "But ignoring your physical well-being is dumb, and you're not dumb. Here—" He took the tray the attendant held. "Thank you, Lisa." He turned to Maeve. "So if you want to be treated like a grown woman, act like one." He set the tray in her lap, then retreated across the cabin.

She resisted the urge to toss the whole thing at his

head. "You are insufferable, you know that?" She lifted a flaky scone. "Okay, watch." She took a bite, then realized how starved she was. She hadn't eaten since breakfast.

He did watch her, the way a lion watches a gazelle. She would worry about being the prey of this very masculine creature, but she was too intent on devouring every morsel. She cleaned the plate and drained her cup, then rose and approached him. "Satisfied?"

His gaze nearly burned her up. "Not even close."

Maeve closed her eyes. Touched one hand to her stomach, now filled with butterflies. "Stop that." She turned on her heel and walked toward the galley.

Behind her echoed the sound of his low chuckle.

It was going to be a long ride back to Dallas.

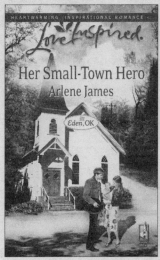

REQUEST YOUR FREE BOOKS!

2 FREE NOVELS PLUS 2 FREE GIFTS!

SPECIAL EDITION®

Life, Love and Family!

YES! Please send me 2 FREE Silhouette Special Edition® novels and my 2 FREE gifts (gifts are worth about $10). After receiving them, if I don't wish to receive any more books, I can return the shipping statement marked "cancel." If I don't cancel, I will receive 6 brand-new novels every month and be billed just $4.24 per book in the U.S. or $4.99 per book in Canada, plus 25¢ shipping and handling per book and applicable taxes, if any*. That's a savings of at least 15% off the cover price! I understand that accepting the 2 free books and gifts places me under no obligation to buy anything. I can always return a shipment and cancel at any time. Even if I never buy another book from Silhouette, the two free books and gifts are mine to keep forever.

235 SDN EEYU   335 SDN EEY6

Name	(PLEASE PRINT)	
Address		Apt. #
City	State/Prov.	Zip/Postal Code

Signature (if under 18, a parent or guardian must sign)

Mail to the **Silhouette Reader Service:**
IN U.S.A.: P.O. Box 1867, Buffalo, NY 14240-1867
IN CANADA: P.O. Box 609, Fort Erie, Ontario L2A 5X3

Not valid to current subscribers of Silhouette Special Edition books.

Want to try two free books from another line?
Call 1-800-873-8635 or visit www.morefreebooks.com.

* Terms and prices subject to change without notice. N.Y. residents add applicable sales tax. Canadian residents will be charged applicable provincial taxes and GST. Offer not valid in Quebec. This offer is limited to one order per household. All orders subject to approval. Credit or debit balances in a customer's account(s) may be offset by any other outstanding balance owed by or to the customer. Please allow 4 to 6 weeks for delivery. Offer available while quantities last.

Your Privacy: Silhouette is committed to protecting your privacy. Our Privacy Policy is available online at www.eHarlequin.com or upon request from the Reader Service. From time to time we make our lists of customers available to reputable third parties who may have a product or service of interest to you. If you would prefer we not share your name and address, please check here. ☐

SSE08R

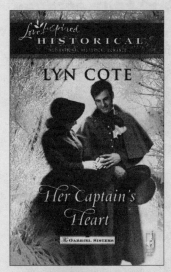